Deadly Flip

A Home Renovator Mystery

by

M. E. Bakos

This book is fiction. All characters, events, and organizations portrayed in this novel are the product of the author's imagination or are used fictitiously. Any resemblance to actual persons—living or dead—is entirely coincidental. The home improvement tips given in DEADLY FLIP are not to be used in lieu of professional help. Author does not make any warranties about the completeness, reliability, and accuracy of this information. Any use of home improvement tips is at the reader's risk.

For information: email mebakos@yahoo.com

ISBN: 979-8-9850770-7-0

Printed in United States of America

For my husband, Joe Sebesta,
and Chipper

CHAPTER 1

"What the heck!" I tugged at the edge of a board in the bottom of the window seat in the second-floor bedroom of my home renovation project. This was my third project in my new profession as a Home Rehab Specialist. I had purchased the house at auction a couple of weeks earlier and was in the midst of the remodel.

"What?" asked my BFF Myra Alexandria Payten, poking her head out of the closet she'd been dusting. She wore a blue denim shirt with sleeves rolled at the cuffs, matching jeans and sported casual work shoes that cost a fortune. Her highlighted hair was freshly styled. She was humoring me with cleaning.

The house was a few blocks from where Myra lived. She was a staunch supporter of my new occupation. It was with her encouragement that I'd decided to flip houses for a living after I was canned from my marketing job at a hospital. She had a passion for home improvement projects, and renewing houses. She had her projects done for her. Me, not so much. She lived in one of the stately mansions facing the "couples" lake in Minneapolis, Minn. It was one of three lakes in the Hiptown area; the other lakes were known as the "singles" and "family" lakes.

She had been over-the-top thrilled when I told her about the project.

"It's a wonderful house, Katelyn! A marvelous opportunity," she'd gushed.

"But I do renovations in Crocus Heights, close to home," I had argued.

"This is a perfect opportunity to expand your horizon. Besides, it's a great deal."

"How do you know?"

"My brother told me the house was up for sale."

"Really? The chief of police follows foreclosures at auction?"

"This one is special. It has a history."

"History?"

"There was an incident, a murder...." As her voice trailed off, she coughed and avoided my stare.

"I don't need bad karma," I warned her.

"The actual murder took place in the garage. The body is gone. No body. No bad karma." She sounded evasive and a little flippant. My guard was up.

"I wouldn't be too sure about that," I said, my eyes narrowed.

"Katelyn, I'd like you to renovate the house." She studied me; her gaze was steady, serious.

"Why don't *you* renovate the house?" I countered. It wasn't like her to push a project. It was weird, especially after my experience with a dead body in my first rehab.

"I'm not the expert that you are in home renovation," she said firmly.

What could I say?

My name is Katelyn Baxter. Most people call me Kate or Katie. I am a Home Rehabilitation Specialist, or a house flipper. It is my passion.

Myra had confidence in me. That meant a lot. If I didn't know better, I would have thought she had a personal interest in the house. But she had grown up in a mansion on Lake Minnetonka, an heir to the Johnson Construction Company.

Like I said, I had been resistant to this rehab. The job was out of my target area of Crocus Heights, where I'd done my first two projects. The craftsman style house needed a lot of TLC along with beaucoup renovating. It needed updating, plumbing, and electrical work. But it was in a good neighborhood with well-kept lawns and a diverse population. Many residents were young college students who lived in the historic brownstone apartment buildings. Homeowners loved the serenity of the city's lakes close to the hustle and bustle of an urban setting.

I bought the house that had one other offer from a tall, thin older woman with a hooked nose, and wispy hair. She sneered and hurried away when she learned I was the lucky bidder.

"Let's take a break," Myra suggested.

"Excellent idea." I gave the board a rest, and we headed to the front porch, discussing what would be next in the renovation. Sheriff Don Williams interrupted our kibitzing. He pulled over, got out of his cruiser, and bounded up the front steps.

"Myra," he nodded.

"Sheriff," she replied. "Out of your jurisdiction, aren't you?" Her hazel eyes twinkled.

"On my way to the office," he said. "Say hello to your brother."

"I will."

He pivoted. "This is your house?" The corners of his eyes crinkled.

"It is, now." I brushed back my dark, unruly hair, and met his cobalt blue eyes, steeling myself against the flutter in my stomach when our eyes locked.

He held out his hand, gripped mine in a firm handshake. "Congratulations, you bought the DJ house."

"DJ?"

"Double jeopardy." His expression held a hint of sympathy mingled with regret. "A young woman, Skye Jones, a tenant, was murdered here about four years ago. The man who killed her stored her body in the garage over the winter. In the spring, he buried her under that planting bed next to the garage." He pointed to the detached, stucco, single-stall garage.

"They charged two men, Ruston Ahoe, the owner/landlord, and Daemon Pleasant, another renter. The tenant took a plea deal and the owner plead not guilty. When the jury acquitted the owner, he confessed to the murder."

"Why would the guy confess after he was acquitted?" I scratched my head, puzzled.

"Don't know. But they released the tenant who took the deal," the sheriff said. "Nothing the owner said implicated him."

"Because he didn't do it?" I asked. "So, nobody paid for this girl's death?"

"They jailed the renter for a short time. The owner couldn't be charged and tried for the same crime again. Double jeopardy." He smiled wryly. "It's the law."

It was March, and the area he indicated was covered with the remains of dead plants and winter debris. The reality that they found a body at the same time of year, years earlier, hit me.

"Oh. My. God." Talk about bad juju.

After Don left, I turned to Myra, "You didn't tell me the part about double jeopardy."

"I said the place had history." She avoided my gaze, picking a piece of lint off her jacket.

I knew I should have done my due diligence and Googled, but the deal had come up quickly. It was a good project, and Myra approved. I had been carried away by the solid home and visions of how I could renew it. But, a murder that no one paid for? A girl lost her life, and the man convicted for the crime gets released? The actual killer is freed?

"You told the sheriff I'd be here this morning, didn't you?"

"Maybe."

"He knew I'd buy the house, didn't he?" I asked.

"Maybe." She smiled coyly.

After finding a body in the attic of my first flip, I was a little sensitive about karma. I didn't want to find a dead body in another renovation, ever. I wanted a simple, straightforward rehab. The place creeped me out.

We went back upstairs to the bedroom to resume work. We passed Wayne Hamer, who was tearing out a wall between the dining room and kitchen.

Wayne is my handyman and neighbor at the townhouses where I live, about a twenty- minute drive through the heart of the city. He is a self-described, recovering alcoholic and has stayed sober for many years. He resembles a hippie with long gray hair and round, metal-framed glasses. He's a wizard with wood.

And, he was freaked. Unlike his usual gregarious manner, the mostly retired carpenter had been quiet outside of occasional bursts of "dang it, anyway," frowning while he tore into the project. Every time the lights flickered, he grumbled. When he checked the circuit breaker panel in the basement, the lights would stop sputtering. An electrician was next on my list to call.

Back at the seat, my head deep in the window bench, I took the board out and examined it.

"The bottom's loose," I muttered. "I'll have to get some wood glue," I said. I wiped the board with a cleaning solution of white vinegar and olive oil and sat back on my heels. I put the board aside and peered inside.

"It's a false bottom!" I spied an object at the bottom and gingerly pulled out a thin, dusty, 5x7 pink, cardboard-backed book. The front of the book had a butterfly in the psychedelic deep blues, pinks, and greens reminiscent of another era. *"Dream,"* was written in ornate swirling script on the cover against a background of deep blue and black, with white stars.

"Looks like a journal," and brushed dust off the book. I opened the cover and read, *"Skye's Diary. DO NOT READ, Personal and Private*, written in flowery handwriting. Circles dotted the *I*'s, and red hearts decorated the corners of the page.

"That's the dead girl's diary! Dang it, Myra, I knew I shouldn't do this project!" I dropped it like a hot potato and stood up.

"It's a wonderful house! Fixed up, it will enhance the neighborhood and boost property values. It's been a few years since the murder." She was firm.

"Four years. Is that enough time for people to forget what happened?"

Myra's rosy complexion paled, and she said in a calm, rational voice, "Skye Jones is dead. Maybe we can find some reason for her life ending so tragically."

"Yeah, the guy got off scot-free. We know that. I tell ya, there was no justice for this girl," I ranted. My blood boiled thinking about the story and the unfairness of the situation.

"It wasn't fair," she agreed. "The law failed Skye Jones."

"Guess it couldn't hurt to read the diary." I picked the journal off the floor and flipped through the thin volume, speculating. A few pages had entries; most were blank.

I sat on the seat. Myra stood at my shoulder. “She was so young. It’s a shame.” She stroked her chin, thoughtful. “The family would want the diary.”

“We should try to find them,” I agreed. “We won’t know anything unless we read it. It’s kind of like finding a wallet. You have to look inside for an ID.”

“It couldn’t hurt.” She considered me for a moment. “Katelyn Baxter. Don’t you dare read the journal without me.”

“I won’t. Promise.” I smiled, closed the book, clutching it to my chest, hiding crossed fingers.

She gazed at me, skeptical.

“Not all of it,” I amended.

“Uh huh. I’ve got to go. I have a date with an exterminator,” Myra said, tossing the dust cloth on the bench, wiping her hands on designer jeans.

“Ooh. Be still my beating heart.” Pretending to swoon, I placed my hand on my chest.

“Yes.” She laughed. “Homeownership doesn’t get any better.”

“Probably not,” I agreed and chuckled.

She stood back and gazed at the moldings, adding, “Isn’t the woodwork wonderful? Such quality craftsmanship. They don’t build them like this anymore. The window bench is a lovely place for a youngster to sit and read and ponder the mysteries of the moon and stars.”

“Uh huh,” I agreed. “It is nice.” I glanced up at her. Her eyes held a faraway look.

“You okay, Myra?”

“Fine.”

“Okay,” I said, quizzically.

“Let’s do Popov’s later,” she said, glancing at her wristwatch. “Oops, I’m late.”

“Sounds like a plan. Five o’clock?” I asked and started paging through the diary.

"That should work."

"I'll walk you out. I need a cup of coffee, and I want to see how Wayne is doing." I placed the diary on the seat and grabbed my mug from the windowsill.

I trailed Myra down the wooden staircase.

On the first floor, we passed the construction dust and newly exposed wall studs where Wayne worked. He wore a sweatband around his head with his gray hair pulled back in a ponytail. A black back brace was fastened around his flannel work shirt. His forehead creased in concentration; he bore the same grim expression he'd had since we started this project. He stopped piling debris in a wheelbarrow and grinned long enough to acknowledge Myra's "Bye, Wayne," with a nod and a wink, then resumed tossing plaster into the container.

At least, that's some kind of smile.

Myra read my expression and lifted her eyebrows in agreement. She could tell Wayne wasn't his jovial self.

"I'll see you later," Myra called out as she strode outside to her black SUV. Clicking her car key, she turned and waved.

I returned to the house, passing Wayne who kept loading the wheelbarrow. I hesitated, shrugged at his stiff back and squared shoulders, and filled my mug with strong coffee from the thermos in the part of the kitchen not yet demolished.

I went upstairs to resume my project. The hardwood floors were in decent shape. My plan was to get up as much dust as possible, clean the floor, then rent a sander to refinish the oak floors. I could save on new flooring, a boon because the house needed rewiring.

The psychedelic butterfly journal beckoned from the bench. I put my coffee mug on the sill, grabbed the book, and sat. *I'll just read a page or two.* The sky was overcast, and I heard a light patter of raindrops at the windowpane as I opened the journal.

I flipped past the page where Skye Jones' girlish swirl declared the diary was off limits and read her first entry. It was dated September 1. She wrote:

"My first week in the city. It is so cool living here. It's a big house. A cute guy who works at the diner lives in the room across from mine. He has brown hair, deep brown eyes, and dimples. He's always smiling. I get a funny feeling when he looks at me. He's just so adorable! My landlord seems pretty cool, too. I told him I was going to school this fall. He thought I meant college. I meant high school. It's my last year. A senior! I'm so pumped. I have to save all my money for food and rent. I don't want to go back home. The kids at school are mean. They tease me about the dumb robbery. It wasn't my fault! I never fit in anyway!"

I stopped reading. She had gotten into trouble and hadn't finished high school. Most kids graduated at eighteen. Justice had failed Skye Jones and her family. Frowning, I closed the diary and placed it on the bench, gulped coffee from my mug, and began cleaning.

Grabbing the vacuum from the hall outside of the bedroom, I vacuumed every corner and crevice of the room. It was close to four o'clock when I finished. I took my cup, tucked the diary under my arm, and headed downstairs.

Wayne lifted the white dust mask that covered his nose.

"Quitting time, Kiddo?" He had most of the wall removed and the debris cleared. The wheelbarrow was filled to the brim. Wayne had called me "Kiddo" from the beginning of our friendship. I liked his nickname. It made me feel younger than my thirty-five years. I admit to twenty-eight. A gal has a right to fudge on her age. Am I right, or am I right?

"Yep. Going to meet Myra later."

"I'll be right behind you. Almost done here." He spied the journal in my hand, "Whatcha got there?"

"Skye Jones' diary. The girl who was killed years back. They found her remains under the planting bed beside the garage."

"You don't say?" His eyes got big and his expression solemn. In a low voice, "Someone was murdered in this house?"

"It happened in the garage." I had considered how to tell Wayne, but was reluctant to pass on any negative information. I needed his help to renovate the house and wasn't sure if he'd work on it with bad vibes attached. I felt a little sheepish about not disclosing. Let's face it, there's never a good time to tell someone there's been a murder where they work.

"That's a bad sign." He rubbed the gray stubble on his chin. "House could be haunted."

"I doubt it. But it's a sad situation." I wasn't sure I believed in ghosts but didn't want Wayne to think I did.

"Thanks for everything today, Wayne." I brushed a lock of hair from my face. "You okay? Lately, you seem a little cranky."

"Nothing I can't handle. Ain't nothing to do with anything here. No ghosts or nothing," Wayne declared, his expression deadpan.

"Because if there's anything you need, let me know," I added. I could have kicked myself. I should have told him when I found out.

"Sure thing." He nodded, picked up the broom, and started sweeping the area.

"Okay." I took him at his word.

I left, vowing to get Wayne to open up, and to search the web for anything else I could find about Skye Jones and the whereabouts of Ruston Ahoe, her killer.

CHAPTER 2

Darting through a light drizzle, I hopped into my new ride, a natty 2000 Ford Festiva. I cranked the engine, switched on the heat, and shivered while I fiddled with the volume of the radio and waited for the car to warm. I'd downsized from the green station wagon I'd had when I renovated the Bluebird Street house in Crocus Heights. That car's engine blew in a car chase with the bad guy.

Borrowing Myra's cushy SUV had been heaven after the wagon died. She had bought a new one with more tech stuff, a rear-view camera, and lord knows what all. But, in my profession, the hatchback was the ticket. It was compact and it came pre-dinged, with a chip in the windshield. I didn't worry about another vehicle getting too close in the tightly packed lakes area of the city. I headed home, maneuvering through the heavy traffic and sped into my driveway, singing along to the music of Maren Morris' "'80's Mercedes."

Mrs. Greta Gilman, one of three residents at the townhomes, stood on the driver's side of a mail truck at the end of the drive. She shielded her strawberry blonde, pixie hairdo from the light rain as the balding, late fiftyish postman handed over her mail. Both were animated with big smiles and kept up their banter after she collected the letters and flyers.

Mrs. Gilman was widowed and spent many hours tending her flowers and shrubbery during the spring, summer, and fall. She and Wayne, my handyman, had spent a lot of time together over the winter, and I called her Gillie with Wayne rather than Mrs. Gilman, as the two were an item. It was too early for the gardening season, and I suspected she watched daytime television while Wayne worked at the renovation.

I gave them a nod, which neither acknowledged, and hurried inside. I stopped at the first door inside the central hall that led to the four townhomes. With a mug in one hand, the diary tucked under my arm, and my handbag heavy on my shoulder, I unlocked my door.

"Yowl." Boots, my rescue cat roommate, leaped from his perch on the back of the sofa, demanding a treat, his tail waving. He weaved around my legs, brushing his body against my jeans. With his black body and white paws, he appeared as if he wore a tuxedo. He had adopted me after I let him in during a storm a year earlier.

"All right, all ready. You're getting fat." I dropped my load on the kitchen table, shook the drops off my jacket and dug into the treat jar on the counter. I felt around the bottom of the jar and made a mental note to get snacks. "This is serious. This is your last treat." I held it out. He wrinkled his nose, snatched the goodie from my hand, and ran off.

I hustled to the bedroom, laid out a clean sweater and jeans, and headed for a shower.

Amid slipping on the sweater, the phone rang, and I dashed to the cordless phone on my nightstand. It was Myra's number on caller ID.

"Hi, Myra?"

"I have more visitors in the attic," She responded, sounding annoyed.

"Pest control didn't get them all?"

"Apparently not. I hear the patter of little feet overhead. And scratching." Her tone was clipped.

"A squirrel?"

"I'm betting on the raccoons," she said tightly. "It's nearly dark. They're nocturnal and come out to play at night. Pest control said it was mating season."

"Great."

An uneasy thought of another creature, a mouse, flitted through my mind, but I kept my mouth shut.

"How would they get into the attic?"

"They must have shimmied up the brick on the house and found an opening."

"And now you hear them playing above your head?"

"Yes," she said, exasperated.

"It's a marvelous house. Can't say that I blame them," I kidded.

"Yes. I have a wonderful home for woodland creatures." She sniffed. Myra lived in a stunning red brick colonial. The grounds were beautifully maintained with lush green grass and well-groomed bushes, courtesy of a landscaping service.

"Sorry."

"It's true," she agreed with a sigh. "I must pass on Popov's. Pest control is coming back. It'll take time to get the critters rounded up."

"That's okay. We'll do it another day."

"Thanks. I must go; the truck is here. I'm sure my neighbors are thrilled," she said, still frustrated. "I'm the hit of the neighborhood."

"They'll understand." I stifled a snicker.

I hung up and gazed at Boots. "It's just you and me." His green eyes gleamed, and he grinned and licked his paws. He knew I'd been stood up on a Friday night.

I thought about calling Don and nixed the idea. Things had been awkward between us since Eddy, my ex, appeared outside my door the evening of our date for the Policeman's Dance. Eddy had picked that night, of all nights, to show up. Eddy and I had been married and divorced shortly after high school, but stayed friends despite parting ways. We were orphans, with no parents or siblings.

Since that evening, Don and I had had a few cordial interactions, but he'd kept his distance and seemed to bond with Eddy a little too much for my comfort. I didn't know what Eddy was up to these days.

I headed to the bathroom, ran a brush through my hair, then padded to the kitchen where I hunted through the refrigerator for dinner.

With my head stuck in the fridge, Boots rubbed against my legs meowing, eager for his dinner. The rain began a steady drum against the patio window in the kitchen.

"Would it be mean to have a pizza delivered in this weather?" A flash of lightning and a crack of thunder sounded. I jumped. "Peanut butter, it is."

I took out the jar and two slices of bread, spread a layer of peanut butter and added more butter to the slices. I poured a glass of chardonnay, setting it on the counter. I opened a can of food for Boots and filled his bowl with fresh water.

Another boom sounded, and I hurried to the patio door. Opening the blinds, I gazed out. The wind whipped the branches of the lilac bushes that bordered Mrs. Gilman's patio and mine. Her kitchen lights illuminated the shrubs. Beyond the bushes, bare branches on willow trees swayed.

"Boots, it's a good night to stay in." I closed the blinds, and gave the cat his chow. Then carried my dinner and wine to the sofa, flipping on the television to the local news. Unable to get Skye's diary out of my thoughts, I finished my sandwich, took my plate to the dishwasher, and returned to turn off the television.

Torn between doing a Google search for Ruston Ahoe and reading Skye's diary, the journal won. I grabbed the thin volume and settled in on the couch, an afghan over my legs. Boots jumped to his favorite place on the sofa.

I opened the journal to the next entry:

September 14. "School is cool. The kids are so different than the stuck-up kids at home. They accept me. It is so fun. But I'm really busy working and going to classes. My job is okay. My feet are sore. The bus was crowded, and I had to stand. I gave up my seat on the bus to an old man on the way home. But my pockets are full of tips. I can pay rent for two days! I bought a burger at Burger World for supper. I ran into the cute guy across the hall when I got home. We work different shifts. He told me to call him DaeDae. He's got such a cute way of talking; he starts every sentence with "hey." "Hey, Skye." "Hey, how's it going?" It's so funny. His eyes are a dreamy soft brown, and he has deep dimples."

Noise coming from the hall interrupted my concentration. I heard the muffled sound of a door shutting in the distance, then all was quiet. It had to be Wayne coming home from the Hiptown renovation. Usually, he rapped at Mrs. Gilman's door, and I would hear the seniors talking. One or the other would ask about dinner plans. I continued reading.

September 23, two o'clock a.m. "I woke to the sound of the doorknob rattling. It scared me. I held my breath and listened. The noise quit, and I fell back asleep. Maybe I was dreaming?"

September 30, two o'clock a.m. "Same noise, same time tonight. I got up, went to the door, cracked it open, and peeked. Nothing! I feel so dumb. It must be some draft or something."

I jumped and gasped when my cell phone rang. Placing the journal on my lap, I reached for the phone on the coffee table. The caller was Sheriff Don, and I tried to sound chill.

"Hello?"

"Hi, Kate," His deep voice drawled. "Is this a good time?"

"Fine. I was reading. Keeping Boots company." It occurred to me that I ought to tell him about the diary, but dismissed the thought.

"What are you reading?"

"Nothing." I didn't know whether the police would want the diary. If they did, I would give it up, but I wasn't ready to hand it over, yet. "Just a book."

"Have you eaten?"

"Barely." I perked up, guilty, thinking about the sandwich and chardonnay combo.

"How about I pick up a pizza, and we can both eat and keep Boots company?"

"Fabulous. Hawaiian?"

"Pineapple on a pizza isn't normal. How about we go half Hawaiian and half everything else?" he asked, laughing.

"You're paying."

"Deal."

While I waited for Don, I powered up the computer and searched for Ruston Ahoe and Skye Jones. Newspaper photos on Google were sketchy at best. A picture of Ruston Ahoe entering the courthouse for the trial showed a man who resembled a church choir boy. He was clean cut, tall, lean, and had a beak of a nose. His brown hair was neatly combed. He turned out in a blue pullover sweater with gray slacks. In contrast, Daemon Pleasant had long, unruly dark brown locks and a full beard. He wore frayed jeans and a plaid flannel shirt and appeared as they took him to jail. They were the same age, twenty-nine at the time of the trial.

"I can see why Daemon might have been charged," I muttered. "Appearances matter. Right Boots? It's why you wear a tuxedo?" He meowed in agreement.

A photo inset of Skye Jones showed a smiling, blue-eyed blonde wearing a jaunty, broad-brimmed straw hat. Long hair trailed from under the hat. She exuded joy and a free spirit.

The news account described the murder as a tenant dispute. A transcript of a 9-1-1 call said Skye had made the call. The dispatcher had recorded Daemon yelling he would kill her if she called the cops. By the time the police came, everyone had settled down. Daemon apparently apologized to Skye, and she didn't press charges. Her family didn't report her as a missing person for several months.

When the cops investigated the premises because of the missing person's report, they found freshly turned dirt beside the garage. They started digging and discovered Skye's body. They charged both men. Daemon's plea deal gave him eight years instead of thirty. Ruston went to trial. With no reason to suspect the landlord, the jury acquitted him. When he got off, he confessed. There was no direct evidence to link Daemon to the murder, and they released him.

I was confused. In Skye's diary, she said she liked Daemon. Something must have happened that summer. Skye was killed in the fall. The ground was frozen, and she had been stored in the garage. She was reportedly buried in the spring after the ground thawed. What happened between Daemon and Skye?

Close to an hour had passed before Don rapped, holding a carryout box from the local pizza parlor. I snatched the container out of his hands. Drying the rain-spotted box, I put it on the table, and took dishes from the cupboard.

He slipped off his jacket, hung the coat on the back of a chair, and sat down, smoothing his damp hair.

"Quite a storm," I said. I set out plates.

"Yeah. Thank goodness the rain has let up a little." He eased into a chair and flipped up the cover on the box.

"Wine?" His eyes were brighter than I remembered.

"I'm a beer man with pizza."

I grabbed a light beer and glass.

"Light?" he squinted at the label.

"Beggars can't be choosers."

"Touché."

I studied the pizza. It was a giant mass of gooey cheese, pepperoni, sausage, and mushroom. "No Hawaiian?"

"Beggars can't be choosers," he quipped.

I frowned, and he laughed. "They were out of pineapple."

"Really?"

"Yep."

"That's okay. I eat any kind of pizza." I scooped out a piece.

We sat and happily munched. When he finished eating, he rose. "I'll be right back."

"Sure." I cleared the table, put the leftovers in a baggie, and dishes in the dishwasher. I heard him exit the bathroom and stop in the living room.

"What's this?" he called.

I thought of the diary left on the coffee table and winced. *Typical cop, always snooping.* I grabbed my glass and sat next to him on the sofa. He held up the volume, wearing a perplexed expression

"It's a diary."

"Yours?" he asked, his eyes twinkling.

"No. It's the diary of the dead girl who was found at the renovation in Hiptown."

"Is this what you were reading?"

"Yes." I squirmed.

"Where d'you find it?"

"Hidden in the false bottom of a built-in bench in her bedroom. A board came loose while I was cleaning and the diary was tucked underneath."

"Is that so." He let out a low whistle, immediately attentive. "Anything important in it?" He studied my expression.

"I don't know. I just started reading it." I shrugged, and added, "I didn't think the police would need it. The case is closed."

"Probably not." He fingered the journal. "Ruston Ahoe was cunning. If there's anything in here that hints at any other crimes, you need to turn it over." He warned me with a stern glance. "No private investigating."

"I will. Nothing yet." I nodded.

"The family would probably want the journal."

"That's what Myra said."

"How is she?" I relaxed with his attention diverted from the diary. Boots leaped up and sniffed the sheriff, curious.

"Good. She has a pest problem right now. Raccoons. We were going to meet up tonight, but she had to cancel."

"Be sure to tell her I said 'hi.'"

"I will." At times I wondered if there was chemistry between the sheriff and Myra. She claimed not. I took her at her word. He was ten years her junior and ten years my senior, and a hunk.

He stood up, leaned over, and brushed his lips softly against mine. "I should go. Early day tomorrow."

"Okay," I murmured, flushed from the kiss and flustered by the warmth of his body. We were at a standoff. That icky unsure stage. Were we dating, or not? Did he care or not?

"Thanks for the company. I'll let myself out. Bye, Boots." He grabbed his jacket and went for the exit. The cat was snuggled in a corner of the couch, licking his paws. He stopped long enough to give the sheriff a stare, then kept grooming.

"I'll see if I can find where Skye Jones' family is." He slipped on his coat. "If you read anything suspicious, let me know."

"Sure." I nodded and met him at the door. "Good night, Sheriff."

"It's Don." He smiled, leaned over, and his lips brushed my forehead.

What the heck kind of kiss is that?

My face flushed; I watched him leave. My mind drifted to the evening of the shindig. I had worn a slinky, black cocktail dress, and he was decked out in a dark gray suit. He looked awesome.

About to leave for the dance, he had planted a kiss on my lips that made me swoon. It was then Eddy chose that exact moment to visit.

"Wifey, are you in there?" Eddy had yelled, at the same moment the sheriff kissed me. I nearly fell over.

"Wifey?" Don asked. His voice low, eyebrow arched.

"It's complicated." I threw open the door, ready to light into Eddy.

"Don, this is my ex, Eddy."

The men studied each other. Don smiled, and Eddy appeared surprised, but recovered quickly.

"What do you want, Eddy?" I demanded. An alarm bell sounded in my mind, and the song "You Look Good" by Lady Antebellum echoed in my head. He was clean-shaven, his dark hair combed, with one careless lock over his forehead. He wore his best blue jeans and a dress shirt. I ignored the sparkle in his brown eyes as I contrasted the men. Eddy with his boyish charm, and Don with an easy smile, trim blond hair with a touch of silver, and cobalt blue eyes, dressed to the nines.

"Are you going out, Katie?" Eddy asked. He held a huge bouquet.

"What's that?" I asked suspiciously, ignoring his question.

"Roses for you." He thrust the bundle of red roses towards me.

"Why?" I took the flowers. Fresh flowers were my soft spot, and I brought the bouquet to my nose and sniffed.

"Ahem." Don cleared his throat. "Katelyn, if this is a bad time..."

"No!" I pivoted. "It's fine!"

"Just cuz, Katie," Eddy said and shrugged, his eyes gleamed. "You look great!"

"I can go," Don said smoothly, reaching for the door knob.

"No!" I stopped him, putting my hand on his shoulder.

"Say, is that your red Corvette, the ragtop, out there?" Eddy faced him. "It's wicked cool! 1985?"

"Yes. I refurbished it," Don said, relaxing, beaming.

"Awesome! How fast does it go?" I was mute while Eddy asked questions like an awestruck teenager.

"Thank you. I've had it up to 120 mph, but that's off the record. The factory specs say it's good for 150." He grinned. "I'll take you out sometime."

"Terrific! That'd be great." Eddy smiled. "I'll see you, Katie." He spun on his heels and strolled out of the building. All the while, the words from that blasted song played in my brain.

"Seems like a likeable guy. It didn't work out?" Don asked.

"No. We were young and immature."

Snapping back to the present, I shut the door firmly, my blood pressure rising. Frustrated, I muttered, "I may as well howl at the moon." The storm picked up, with several crashes of thunder.

"Serves you right," I muttered. He would get drenched before he got to his car.

CHAPTER 3

The next morning, I sat at the kitchen table, dressed in sweatshirt and jeans, and scanned my list of 'to do' items on a legal pad. I was on my third cup of hazelnut java. Recently, I had decided I was in a rut and would branch out from my standard Colombian blend by trying different coffees, so hazelnut it was.

I mulled over the sheriff's admonition to tell him if anything caught my attention in Skye Jones' diary. He had a lot of nerve, considering he'd told me about the double jeopardy situation after I'd bought the house. Of course, he couldn't know I'd get the rehab. Hiptown was in the next county over, out of his jurisdiction. Still, I grumbled to myself, "Myra suggested I might buy it. He knew I flipped houses for a living." Okay. I was a little peeved about his disappearing act.

The rain had continued overnight and ratcheted to a steady downpour. They projected the storm to last through the weekend. It had taken a major effort to get dressed and focus on the tasks at hand. It was Friday. I usually took Fridays to get supplies, do the finances, and have a little fun. Wayne and I were putting in extra time to finish the project and get away from the negative energy that permeated the atmosphere.

Rat-a-tat-tat! came the knock at the door. From the sound and pattern, it was the handyman. He was prompt, checking in before work.

With mug in hand, I let him in.

“Ready, Kiddo?” He wore a blue jean jacket with a gray hoodie underneath and grungy blue jeans. He appeared tired, with puffy circles under his eyes, the darkness magnified by his round, gold metal-rimmed glasses. He was unshaven.

“Are you ready?” I asked, adding. “You look tired.”

“Couldn’t sleep. Too danged noisy with the storm.”

“Same here,” I said. “You sure you’re up to this today?”

“Yep.” He sniffed the aroma of the coffee. “Got a to-go cup?”

“Of course!” I took out a travel cup and filled it. “Do you have the thermos?”

“Nuts! Forgot it at the job.”

“I’ll get it filled at the Coffee Mill later.” The shop was our favorite, and within walking distance of the house.

He took a deep drink, his expression thoughtful, as he fingered the mug.

“We got a serious problem with the wiring. I’ve flipped every circuit, again and again, the lights keep flickering. It’s gotta be a dang short.”

“I know, Wayne. I’ll get an electrician. It’s annoying, but if we can keep working, it’ll cut the time for the renovation.”

“Sure. I know where you’re coming from. Time is money. Heck, I could fix it.”

“Be great if you could.” I added, “Don’t want you to get hurt.”

"Uh huh." He took a gulp of coffee and avoided my gaze. He focused on the gray day and the drizzle outside the patio slider.

I grabbed my black jacket from the hall closet. "Is there something else?" I asked, my stomach churning as I slipped on the coat. *Whatever it is, don't let it be expensive. I hope he's not going to quit on me.*

"Does Gillie seem a mite 'off'?'" He glanced at me and shuffled his feet, then stared at the floor. He studied his tan boots and his mouth twitched as if he wanted to say more.

"'Off'? What do you mean?" I zipped the jacket.

"She doesn't want to do much these days."

"Oh." I thought back to when I'd seen her at the mail truck. A little alarm sounded in my mind.

"She's gearing up for the garden for Ariel with Broccoli man. (His name was Bob, but I dubbed him Broccoli man due to an incident with rotting vegetables). Waiting on seeds for the spring planting. She orders through the mail," I offered. *Let's hope that's all there is to it.*

"That's probably it. I'd better get going." Relieved, he headed to the exit.

"I'll see you there."

"You betcha," he said, and let himself out.

After Ariel, another neighbor who was strangled by her boyfriend in her townhouse, died, her family had decided to redo her place. Wayne and I had done the renovation. Presently, the unit sat empty; it was on the far side of Mrs. Gilman's townhouse. Part of Ariel's family's wishes was to establish a memorial garden by the townhome. Mrs. Gilman and Bob would start the garden this spring.

Although plans were underway, it was too early for gardening. The spring rains would wash away the rest of winter. I had no doubt the two would design and nurture a great garden, and the project would be a success.

I retrieved my mug, filled it for the road, and grabbed my bag, about to leave. Hesitating, I detoured to the coffee table, snatched up the diary, tucking the thin volume into my messenger bag.

After a quick stop at the drive-up window at the coffee stand, I parked on the street in front of the renovation. Wayne's white van, whom he'd named *Matilda,* sat in the driveway. Parking in this neighborhood was always at a premium. Winter restrictions were on during March, and I carefully watched the street signs. I was no stranger to the city impound lot.

I trekked up the drive beside Matilda and let myself in the back door that led into the kitchen. I filled the thermos with the fresh java. Leaving my cup by the thermos, I stepped past a metal toolbox overflowing with hammers, screwdrivers, and nails.

Wayne nodded from where he'd taken out a wall that separated the kitchen from the dining and living rooms. Construction dust covered the place. The gloomy daylight necessitated task lighting and Wayne had hooked up a cage light to illuminate the work area. All the lights blinked. I shrugged, returned his greeting, and headed upstairs to finish cleaning the bedrooms. I made a quick check of Skye Jones' room and proceeded to the second bedroom, past the full bath separating the bedrooms.

I toted my cleaning materials from where I'd left them in the hall a day earlier. Gray skies were visible from the room's lone window. This was the room where Daemon Pleasant had stayed, a fact gleaned from Skye's diary. The bedroom was narrow and long, about the same size as Skye's. The far wall was divided into two parts, one space held a small closet. The space between the outside wall and the closet formed an alcove with enough area for a desk.

I dropped my cleaning supplies, grabbed the dust mop, and started wiping the walls. While I worked, I considered colors that would freshen the sturdy bungalow. I wanted lighter shades of the earth tone colors that dominated the era. Keep the space bright and reflect the period. City records said the home was built in 1914, smack dab in the middle of the craftsman' era, which ended around the start of the Great Depression in 1929.

I heard a noise and felt a gust of wind. I quit dusting the walls and ceiling. Frowning, I listened.

Bam. Click. Bam.

I went to investigate. The door to Skye's old room was shut. I twisted the knob and peered in. Nothing.

Had Wayne opened a door downstairs? An open door could create a draft on the second floor. Puzzled, I went downstairs to where he worked. He had started wearing earplugs on the job. His back was to me while he loaded the wheelbarrow. Both the back and front doors were shut.

I gauged the amount of debris in the wheelbarrow. It was about half full. Doubtful he'd emptied it.

I tapped him on the shoulder. Startled, he whirled to face me. Plucking out an earplug, "Huh? Whew, you scared me."

"Sorry. Did you open a door?"

"Nope. Haven't got that far." His eyes widened. "You heard it, too?"

"What?"

"Sounds like doors slamming. That's why I put in earplugs, blocks out the banging noises. Creeps me out."

"Maybe, there's a draft somewhere? How about the basement?"

"Kiddo, you look all you want. I haven't had any doors or windows open." He shrugged and spread his hands as if giving up.

"There has to be an explanation. Doors don't open and shut by themselves," I insisted. "I'll check."

He shook his head, dropped the foam plugs in his top shirt pocket and kept loading the cart.

I opened the cellar door, flipped the light switch, and tiptoed down the narrow stairwell. It was a tight fit. At the bottom, behind the staircase, sat a hot water tank. Mounted on the wall beside the heating system was a circuit breaker cabinet, an update. Most homes from the era had fuses.

To the right of the staircase was a dark room that may have held the household's home-canned goods. An old washer and dryer were across the steps. A laundry tub was next to the washer. Above the appliances was a small window, one of two in the long narrow space. Both windows were covered with dust and cobwebs. I went to the window closest to the washer/dryer and heard a click. The room went dark.

"Wayne!" I gasped.

"Sorry! I thought you were done." The dim bulb at the threshold lit up.

"Criminy," I muttered. "This place wigs me out, too." I'd seen enough. The grimy windows looked as if they had not been touched in decades. I lost my nerve to investigate the canned goods storage area and trekked upstairs. I hadn't found the source of the draft, and that annoyed me. Maybe there was an open window in Skye's bedroom. I hadn't seen anything earlier in my first check. With the rain, it seemed unlikely, but I continued to her old room to investigate.

There it was. Hidden from view of the doorway, a window sash was up about four inches.

"I don't remember opening this." I lowered the sash and frowned. It hadn't been high enough to let rain in. "Must have been Myra."

Wayne had followed me upstairs and watched from the doorway. "Found the culprit, huh?" He scratched his head and shrugged.

"Yep. Myra must have opened it yesterday." I observed Wayne. His face was ashen.

"You're sure you want to work today?"

"Could use a smoke break," he added, "Between the windows, dang lights, and noises, house kind of gets to me."

"I'll meet you outside. I need a break too."

I filled my mug with the fresh brew. Outside on the porch, the sky was still gray and a light rain started. We watched the drizzle in companionable silence.

Wayne lit up, took a drag from a Camel cigarette and blew out smoke. The fumes made my eyes water, and I moved out of its path.

He saw my maneuver. "Yeah. Gillie wants me to quit, too. Makes her crazy, the smell."

"It's a tough habit to break," I said, with a sympathetic smile.

He exhaled. "That's just part of it."

"Oh?"

"She doesn't think I can make a commitment. Get married. Called me commitment-phobic. Big words." He snorted and had another puff.

"Oh." I was mildly surprised that the relationship between the seniors had gotten serious.

"Says we aren't getting any younger. Thinks we should tie the knot. Make it legal."

"Okay." I tried to sound neutral.

"What do ya think?"

I groaned. "I'm not the person to ask for marriage advice. I've been married twice."

"Yeah. I done it once. Almost killed me when we broke up," he grumbled. "Hard on the kid and me." He had a daughter in Michigan he saw a few times a year.

"Gillie knows that?"

"Yep. She's been avoiding me ever since." He puffed on his cigarette.

"I'm sorry. Maybe she needs time to think."

"Huh! I've seen the way she acts around that mailman."

"It's probably nothing," I remembered how her face lit up talking to the postman, and squirmed. I was glad I hadn't said anything and hoped it was nothing. "You know me how it is with me and Eddy," and asked, "By the way, you didn't say anything to Eddy about Sheriff Don inviting me to the Policeman's Dance?"

"Oh." He chuckled and winked. "Might have."

"Wayne!" I chided.

He took another drag of his smoke. "That Eddy loves you. You can see it every time he looks at you."

"Been there, done that." I grimaced.

"Just saying." He chuckled. "How's it going with the lawman?"

"He gets along with Eddy better than I do."

"Ya saying it's a bromance?" He guffawed.

"Appears so. Grrrr." I shook my head.

The wind picked up, and the sky darkened with thick, heavy clouds. Within minutes, the wind whipped at the porch. Wayne stubbed out his cigarette on the sole of his shoe. We bolted indoors.

Inside, we paused, gasping from the sudden fierceness of the storm. The living room light sputtered and died out. Gradually, our vision adjusted to the dim lighting, and we shivered in the cool house.

"Dang it, anyway," He groused. "I'll look at the circuits, again." He grabbed the flashlight from the counter and hurried to the cellar. I followed him to the top of the stairs and waited while he tried different breakers. When the lights came on, I breathed a sigh of relief.

"We're good!" I called.

"You might want to come down here and see this," Wayne yelled.

"Okay." Puzzled, I started down.

I was halfway down the tight space when he called out, "Or not?"

"What is it?" My voice quivered, and I stopped behind him.

He stood on the bottom step and pointed in the direction of the fruit cellar. A small furry figure lay at the entrance of the room, bloated with death.

"Is that a mouse?" I whispered.

"Yep. You got mice problems."

"Eek!" I spun around and hurried upstairs. Dead rodents made my knees go weak.

"That's okay, I'll get the bugger. Just get me a plastic bag!"

I grabbed a trash bag and pitched it.

"Got it." I heard rustling sounds. He trotted from the cellar, carrying the package with the offending rodent. Holding it at an arm's length, he strode through the room. At the exit, he threw up his hood and ran the package to the dumpster. He returned, grumbling, "Whew. It's bad out there. You didn't see the little bugger down there earlier?"

"No!" I shuddered.

"Well, don't matter none. Could be the reason the wire is shorting out. Mice chewing on the electrical wires."

"I'll call in an exterminator. Tomorrow, I'll bring Boots. See if he can catch any mice. Thanks for doing that, Wayne."

"All part of the job." He chuckled.

CHAPTER 4

The rain kept up its steady drumming during my stops on the way home. My first stop was the local hardware store, where I loaded up on traps and anything else that appeared as if it would eliminate mice. I picked up a couple of cans of gap filler to fill any spaces around the foundation. I shuddered at the thought that there was more than one, ready to move in and start a family.

My next stop was a Big Mart. I grabbed some provisions, a new coffee—French Roast—, bananas, bread, and peanut butter. I bought extra treats for Boots. He didn't know it yet, but he would earn his keep by catching mice.

At home, with my provisions put away and Boots fed, I called Myra. "What happened with the raccoons?"

"They're gone. Relocated to a more suitable environment."

"Uh huh." I didn't want to know where they put the little critters. "How much does an exterminator run?"

When she told me, I mentally tallied my budget. "I'll get rid of mice the old-fashioned way, Boots, and traps." I told her about my dead mouse in the basement.

"Not good, a mouse in the house." She groaned.

"Nope."

"There's probably more," she said.

"Yep."

"Hopefully, they haven't found their way upstairs."

"One problem at a time, Myra." I had considered that possibility but wasn't ready to go there.

"How about a bite at Popov's tonight?" she asked. "I haven't seen Skye's diary."

I brightened at the prospect of hot food and warm beverages on a rainy night. "Sounds good. Seven?"

"See you there."

I showered and changed into my best blue jeans and a red sweater. I needed something bright. After taking a brush to my hair, I pulled it back in a ponytail and sprayed my bangs. It was a bad hair day, and I'd have to tough it out with the rain. My umbrella was God knows where. Shrugging into my jacket, I grabbed my bag, checking for the thin volume. It remained secure in my purse, through the chaos of finding the mouse, drafts, and flickering lights.

"We'll have quality time, tomorrow," I said to the cat as he glared from the sofa, his tail swishing. He wasn't satisfied by a random kitty treat. After leaving Boots fresh water, I headed out, using my handbag to shield my hair as I ran to my car.

I strolled into the restaurant, flicking raindrops with five minutes to spare. Ivan and Maggie, the restaurant owners, stood behind the cash register, deep in conversation. They waved me to the hostess, a cranky, no-nonsense brunette who ruled the restaurant wait staff.

"This way," she snipped. She wove between tables filled with laughing patrons.

"A booth, if possible." She stiffly pivoted from a table, menu under her arm, and stalked to a booth next to the kitchen bussing cart. From the set of her chin, I dared not ask for a booth away from the kitchen din. I slid in and smiled. "Thanks." If the food wasn't so yummy at Popov's, I'd find another restaurant.

Myra spotted me from the hostess station. She smiled and waved. Her rain coat was stylish and fresh, and her hair had weathered the storm. I wondered how she pulled it off.

"Quite a day," she breezed, setting her designer bag on the seat beside her. "Don't let me forget my umbrella. I left it in the entry."

"Uh huh. Good idea, umbrella." I nodded. "I'm starved."

"Let's order. I'll have the usual." She laid down the menu and looked for the waitress. "Oh, it's her," she said brightly.

"Yes. It is." I added my menu to hers, placed it at the end of the table, and the touchy brunette showed up. It appeared she was filling in for an absent server that day. We ordered our burgers with everything along with a glass of chardonnay and waited. The wine appeared, and we each took a swallow.

"So, the diary?" She asked and put her glass down.

I plucked the thin book from my purse. "So far, what stands out is that she's very young, and she has her eye on the housemate, Daemon Pleasant." I offered the journal. "I've read a few of the entries. Don said the same thing you did; the family would want the diary."

"You've seen the sheriff?" she asked with a smile and a raised brow.

"Yes. He says, 'hi.' And for you to tell your brother the same."

"Spill it. Tell me everything." She put the book aside, gazed at me expectantly. "How did it go?"

"Not much to tell. He brought a pizza. We ate. He left." My face flushed with the memory of his light kiss and abrupt departure.

"He'll come around. He's such a nice man. You two would make a perfect couple." She smiled confidently.

"Myra. I think he just wants to be friends." I groaned, shaking my head.

"Harrumph. Let's read the diary."

"Let's." I nodded, happy to drop the discussion about the sheriff. Myra could be a little pushy. I wasn't sure where Don and I were going, or *if*, we were going.

She picked up the volume and opened it, scanning the first entries. Her eyebrows raised, she stared over at me, "she hasn't finished high school."

"Nope."

"Doesn't like her school," she resumed reading.

"Most kids don't like high school, do they?" I piped in.

"Most of the girls liked the home economics programs, sewing, and cooking." Myra had taught at a public high school before she took early retirement. She was financially comfortable with a fortune made from investments in real estate and her deceased husband's stake in his family's department stores.

"Yeah. I think those subjects may be different. Outside of classes, school could be a jungle. Kids were mean if you weren't part of their clique. She claims she didn't fit in."

"She planned to save enough money from her waitressing job to live in the city and finish school." Myra gasped as she scanned the page. "Where were her parents?"

"She doesn't say much about her family. She talks more about Daemon. And things that go bump in the night." I sipped wine and shook my head.

"She hears noises?"

"Yes."

"Could be stress. That's a lot for a young girl to take on," she said. She flipped through the pages.

"Maybe." I thought about the curious events that day at the house, the flickering lights, the draft, and the sound of doors closing. I recalled Wayne's jitters and shrugged.

I was about to ask her if she had opened a window in Skye's room, when she questioned, "You have a mouse?"

"Yep. I'm putting Boots to work tomorrow." I chuckled.

"He'll have fun with that." She laughed. "If you need the name of an exterminator, let me know."

"I'll try traps and Boots, first. Plug up holes."

"Perfectly fine," she agreed, nodding as she took a sip of wine. Our food arrived, and we dug into the mammoth burgers.

"Raccoons are a special problem," I said, between bites of food.

"They are indeed." She laughed. "They're gone now. All openings have been plugged according to Exterminators R Us."

"Excellent." After eating the last morsel, I sat back.

Myra opened the diary. She turned a few pages and gasped, "Did you see this?"

"No. What?" I leaned over.

"She says Ruston surprised her in the kitchen and kissed her. The passage is dated October 15."

"I don't know what to do. I woke and heard the noises again. I couldn't get back to sleep. Rusty, he told me to call him that, snuck up on me while I was getting a glass for milk. He grabbed me by the shoulders, flipped me around, and kissed me. He stuck his tongue down my throat. It was horrible. He smelled like stale cigarettes and beer. Yuck!"

Myra grimaced, gazed at me. "That poor girl."

"Oh, boy," I groaned. "What else does it say?"

She read:

"I ran back to my room and shut the door. I propped my desk chair under the doorknob. I'm scared. DaeDae is working. I wish he was here."

"That's terrible." I flinched. "What else?"

"He rattled the knob, called my name, moaned, and finally walked away. He must shake the doorknob in the middle of the night. The noise wakes me. I'm so scared. I'll get a knife, maybe. I can't wait for DaeDae to get here. When he gets home, I'll talk to him. He'll know what to do." She turned the page.

"The news account says she called the police on Daemon," I said, puzzled. "Not Ruston."

"Odd. Maybe the dispatcher misheard? Maybe the police record is wrong? We know she doesn't want to go home. There must have been some problems in the family if they didn't report her missing for several months." She shook her head." Poor girl."

"She sounds pretty level-headed if she's working, saving her money, and living on her own. It might have worked, except for Ruston." I frowned, thinking about the entry. "What does she say next?"

Myra flipped to the next entry. "It's dated October 21, 2:30 a.m." She glanced at me:

"I took the butcher knife from the kitchen and hid it under my pillow. Rusty will be sorry if he tries anything funny. Daemon says Rusty was drunk. He said he would talk to him. It must have worked because he hasn't done anything for a week. I haven't heard any noises. But I think I'm losing it. I woke up at 2:00 a.m. I swear I hear someone crying. It was distant, downstairs, or coming from the basement. Probably just a dream. I'm really stressed. Work is hard. My manager yelled at me today."

"What else?"

"Nothing. That's it." She rifled through the rest of the pages, and looked at me. "That's the last entry. It's dated about six months before she was found."

I reached for the diary and tucked the book in my shoulder bag, meeting Myra's gaze.

"Wow." I gulped. "That could have been the night Ruston Ahoe killed her."

CHAPTER 5

I hightailed it to the Hiptown rehab Saturday morning. It was another gray day, and I took an extra strong cup of java in my travel mug.

Boots sat in his carrier, indignant at having his sleep routine interrupted. He howled from the hatch while I scored a parking place in front of the house. Wayne had parked in the drive. I hopped out and opened the back.

"It's okay." I tried to soothe the animal. I gave him a treat from the baggie stuffed into my handbag. Mollified, he ate it. "Not too many. There's something better inside."

Momentarily quiet, the black cat sat on his haunches cowering, his front paws braced. I flung the straps of my bag over my shoulder and lifted out the cage and headed inside.

Wayne was mudding the seams of the new drywall with paper and compound. He stopped, trowel in hand.

"See ya brought in the big guns today." He nodded at Boots, who let out another yowl. "This the guy who's gonna get rid of the rodents?"

"No doubt about it!" I deposited the carrier and dropped my purse on the counter. "I'll let him get comfortable first."

Boots sat immobile, glaring from the back of the crate as I undid the latch.

"I'll give him a little time, then show him the basement." He wasn't buying it and hissed. I placed a treat in his cage to coax him out.

"Sure." Wayne snickered and resumed smoothing the drywall seams. Deep in thought, he appeared glum as he applied compound. His gray hair was pulled back in a braid and he didn't wear earplugs.

I considered asking about Gillie but decided not to. If they hadn't made plans for the evening and that irritated him, I didn't want to raise the subject. I returned to the car to get my mug of extra strong brew and grabbed the plastic bag that held traps and a small jar of peanut butter brought as bait.

Back inside, Boots stayed at the rear of the kennel, curled up as far away from the exit as possible, glowering. I stooped in front of the cage and dangled a treat.

"Okay, Boots, this is outside of your job description, but I need your special skill set to handle a sticky situation," I said.

With my luck, I had rescued the only cat in the county that didn't catch mice. I left the treat and closed the crate. I grabbed my bag of pest control supplies and the carrier.

"Wayne, I'm taking Boots to the basement."

"Sure thing." He nodded, guffawing as he continued working.

Carefully, I descended the narrow staircase. At the landing, I set the carrier down and unlatched the opening. The cat stood, hissed, his back raised, tail up, pressed against the far end.

"You got up. I guess that's progress." I studied the kitty. The cellar smelled damp from the rain, and I shuddered thinking about what might lurk in the shadows as I prepared the snares. I wore disposable gloves as I spooned a bit of spread on the trap and set the trigger mechanism. *I hope Wayne is still on board with mouse disposal.*

Boots sniffed the air. He sat, staring at a point beyond my shoulder to the entrance of the fruit cellar. I followed his gaze to see if I could see anything. Nothing.

I heard Wayne's footfalls on the stairs.

"How's it going?" He joined me.

"Not so good." I frowned at Boots. Together, we viewed the animal.

"He sees something," I said, puzzled.

"Sure does," he agreed.

"Do you see anything?" My eyes strained in the dimly lit area, shivering.

"Nope. Gives me the heebie-jeebies, though."

Boots' eyes glittered green as he stared. His whiskers flicked as he glared at the entry to the room beyond us. The cement wall had been patched, the surface uneven and flaking. A cobweb clung to a corner of the doorway.

"What do you think?" I asked after a couple of minutes.

"I ain't never seen a cat act like this," he said. "Come on, kitty. There's some good eating to be had." He squatted next to the cage and cooed. The cat's attention never wavered from an invisible object. He hissed again, his back hunched and green eyes fixed.

"I think Boots here doesn't do mice or basements." He laughed, a tinge of uneasiness coloring his voice. He jabbed at his glasses, pushing them higher on the bridge of his nose.

"I'll put out the traps and forget about Boots catching mice," I said. "Will you pick up any sprung traps?" My stomach churned. Boot's behavior gave me the willies. I decided to clear out of the cellar.

"You betcha," he said, and nodded. "I'll be upstairs." He took the wooden treads two at a time.

I inhaled, calmed my nerves and steadied my hands as I finished baiting the contraptions and placed them by the washer, dryer, the heating system, and open pathways. Boots stayed quiet while I worked. When I finished, I closed his cage and hauled it upstairs.

"Yowl!" Boots protested as I stepped on the first floor. I yelled over his howls, "Wayne, I'm taking Boots home." I snatched my bag and carried the crate to the car. Stowing the cage in the hatch, I dropped a treat. He nibbled on his snack, blessedly quiet. His challenge was over, and he could relax.

Behind the wheel, I cranked the engine, flipped the visor down and watched the cat through the vanity mirror. "That's all you got? You don't do rodent duty?" He wrinkled his nose. I snorted, flipped the visor up, and drove off.

When I pulled into the drive at the townhomes. Gillie was at the mail truck. With a stab of guilt, I recalled what Wayne had said about her and the mailman. I hadn't told him I'd seen the couple laughing, appearing cozy. I wouldn't add to his angst and it was probably innocent. I avoided staring at the pair, but she had a blush to her complexion, and the ordinarily quiet woman was animated as she spoke to the driver.

I took out the cage. The cat was quiet. After closing the hatch, I glanced over to see Mrs. Gilman waving at the departing postal truck, clutching her mail.

Good time to get the mail. Leaving the carrier at the car, I ambled to the boxes for the day's delivery.

"Hi, Mrs. Gilman."

"Katelyn." She nodded and gave a small smile, "Another gloomy day, isn't it?" She evaded my gaze, threw the hood up on her down jacket, and hurried to the townhomes. The spring weather was too cold for her normal attire of hoodie and sweatpants.

"Yep, it's been a stretch of miserable weather," I called after her. *That's a guilty look if I've ever seen one.* I plucked my mail from the box and sorted it. *Publishers Clearing House*. I grimaced at the envelope and the bills, returned for Boots, and went inside.

The phone jangled as I blew in. I left the crate, dumped the letters and my bag on the kitchen table, and answered the phone.

"Hi, Kate." My stomach dropped. It was Eddy. It was never a good sign when Eddy called. The rent was due for the Bluebird house in a week. Normally, he'd slip the check under the door, if I wasn't home. He had agreed to rent my first rehab project with a rent-to-own agreement. Buyers were skittish with the economy. Eddy was my best bet, but his track record with employers was marginal. I had hoped the possibility of becoming a homeowner would motivate him to stay gainfully employed.

"What's up?" I braced myself. While I waited for him to speak, I undid the latch to the cage, and the kitty darted to his refuge on the sofa.

"Kate." My stomach sank further. He usually called me "Wifey," if only to annoy me. He used 'Kate,' or 'Katie,' if he was serious. "I'll be late with the rent this month. I can pay half on the first, and the other half later in the month."

"How much later?" Thinking about the mortgage on the home, and the expenses of rehabbing the Hiptown property.

"Should be the fifteenth," he said. "Sorry, Kate. I've had some setbacks this month. Truck needs brakes and new tires."

"Okay, Eddy. It can't be any later. I have a lot going on, too." My blood pressure spiked, and I bit my tongue. He'd never been good at money management. If it were up to him, we'd have been living under a bridge when we were married. He was so darned handsome and easy to get along with that he'd gotten away with most anything during our short, explosive marriage, except for the bimbos.

"Sure, Kate, I'll drop it off, now."

"You can leave it under the door," I said quickly.

"Are you going out?"

"Yep. Gotta go." I didn't want to take a chance on wilting under his charm. On the phone or in person.

"Thanks, Katie, you're the best." His voice was low and sexy.

"Yeah, Eddy." I hung up with a sigh. Part of me still had feelings for him. I'm a mush. He had been my first love. Even after being married to Jake. But my saner self knew better than to rekindle a flame.

I phoned Myra next. "Are you coming to the renovation today?"

"Wouldn't miss it. I'll come about one o'clock, after lunch."

"Bring the telephone number for your exterminator."

"I thought you were doing it the old-fashioned way. A cat and traps?"

"Still doing traps. Boots isn't happy with the mouse hunting plan."

"Too spoiled to hunt?" she asked and chuckled.

"Maybe. Couldn't tell. He wouldn't come out of his crate." He lay curled up on the couch, watching warily.

"I brought him home. He was too freaked."

"Poor kitty," she said.

"He's better off at home." As I watched, he started to relax, closed his eyes. No worse for his trauma. "I have to rent a sander and get back to Hiptown. We'll chat later."

"Sounds good. I'll see you then."

I disconnected and snagged my purse from the table. "You're off the hook, Boots." I headed out.

I stopped at a rental store in Crocus Heights on the way to Hiptown and rented a sander. The selection was awesome. There were different sanders available, depending on the condition of the floors. The store also rented floor edger's, and a sander that slipped under radiators. I figured the standard drum model would do it. A deal at about fifty bucks for four hours. The clerk lifted the machine into my vehicle.

"Good luck," he said, and slammed the hatch.

"Thanks." I drove off, and a vision of smooth floors, ready for new stain, ran through my mind.

At the renovation, I hustled inside and asked Wayne to bring the sander upstairs. He had finished mudding the drywall for the open concept living, dining and kitchen area. The area was greatly changed, and I admired his work.

"This is fabulous! Great job."

"Thanks, Kiddo. I think so, too." He stood back with a proud grin. "Whole lot more room, now."

"Buyers will love it!"

We went to the car, and he hoisted the machine from the hatch.

"This will work," he said.

"Yes." I nodded. The prospect of freshly refinished floors on the second level inspired me.

I got to work. About two hours into sanding the floors, the lights went out, and the house darkened. The drum sander stopped humming.

"Wayne," I called from Skye's old bedroom. I had nearly finished the room and was considering the edger.

"I'll check the breakers," he yelled from the main floor.

While I waited for him to check the circuits, I switched off the machine and withdrew to the window, gazing at a steady downpour. While I was working, the skies had opened, and gray clouds had given way to a steady rain. Through the shower, I spotted Myra parking her black SUV behind Wayne's van. She opened her door, flipped open a black umbrella, hopped out, and strolled to the house. I glimpsed her tan trench coat and new blue jeans.

Looks like she will be on dusting duty again. Her work clothes could be my out-on-the-town outfit. I went down to meet her and waited at the front entry.

"Hello!" She caught her breath, stopping on the porch. She shook her umbrella, left it in a corner and breezed in. Frowning, she commented, "It's a little dark."

"Electricity is out. Wayne is trying the circuit breakers." The lights blinked on. "Must have known you were coming," I quipped. Wayne emerged from the basement, a flashlight in hand.

"We need an electrician. Something is making it trip. It's not normal. Yo, Myra," he said and left the light on the counter.

"Wayne, this is wonderful." Myra gazed at the progress and exclaimed, "It makes the area appear much larger."

"Thanks. Not bad, if I do say so myself." He grinned.

"I'll show you what I've done." I smiled at Wayne as we left him to his chores and headed upstairs.

"Have you noticed how bad the storm is getting out there?" Myra asked as she followed me.

"It's supposed to rain all week. Good time to be doing this project, huh?"

"You're right." She viewed the area. "Great job. This is going to make the floors like new. You're almost done in here," she said, as she left her belongings in the closet.

"Yes."

"Let's see the other bedroom."

"I'll lead the way." We left Skye's room and walked to the second bedroom, passing the main bathroom.

"This space is a little smaller. How long do you have the machine?" she asked.

"About two more hours. That should take care of the bulk of the heavy sanding. Then, I'll rent an edger, clean up the ends."

"Okay." She peered through the rain splattered window. "Katelyn, there's a strange-looking man over there!"

"Where?" I stood behind her and scanned the yard. A man wearing a beanie hat and a vintage khaki, army-style jacket, yanked his coat collar up as he trotted through the backyard.

"He's trespassing. Taking a shortcut to the next street," I said. As if he sensed he was being observed, the man glared up at the second-story window and took off running.

"That's a funny outfit," she said, frowning.

"Funny looking guy. Did you see the honker and goatee on that dude?" I asked. "Do men wear goatees anymore?"

"Some men do. It takes all kinds." Myra chuckled.

"I guess it does," I laughed, the sight of the trespasser still imprinted on my mind. *Such an odd fellow.*

"I'll dust," Myra announced.

"Unless you want to try the sander?" Her eyes widened, and I giggled.

"No, that outfit does not do sanding," I said, with a grin. I wore my usual frayed blue jeans and a gray sweatshirt. "I'd better get moving if I want to return the machine in time."

I hurried back to Skye's old room. Myra grabbed the duster and proceeded cleaning Daemon's former room. We switched rooms once I finished sanding.

At 2:45 p.m., I shut off the machine and wrapped the cord, ready to get Wayne's help loading it.

"Whew, let's call it a day, Myra," I said, as we met in the hall outside the bedrooms.

"Yes. I must go. I have tickets to the opera tonight."

"Sounds interesting." My musical tastes ran to country and classic rock music. Maybe I would put opera on my bucket list. "Did you shut all the windows?"

"I didn't open a window. Too much rain."

"Last time you dusted; a window was left open in Skye's old room." I recalled the draft.

"I've never opened windows in any of the rooms," she insisted.

"Okay?" I shrugged and scratched my head. "It must have been Wayne."

"Probably," she said, as she disappeared into the bedroom, returning with her coat and purse.

"Wayne! Little help, please?" I called from the top of the staircase.

"Sure thing." He glanced at me. His hood up was up, he'd been waiting for me to finish and he bounded up the stairs.

I followed him as he lifted the sander down the steps. On the main floor, I gathered my keys, handbag, and jacket ready to leave. Myra dug keys from her purse and retrieved her umbrella, preparing to move her SUV from behind Wayne's van.

"Found two little critters in the basement," Wayne said, pausing at the front exit, as we braced ourselves to go into the rain.

"Two mice?" I asked, grimacing.

"Yep."

"Perfect," Myra said, and groaned. "Too bad Boots doesn't hunt mice."

"Yeah. I didn't put it in his job description," I said.

"Ain't no way Boots will go back to that cellar. That's the truth," Wayne said and chuckled. His hands rested on the machine's handle, ready to take the it outside.

"What do you mean?" Myra asked.

"He wouldn't budge, just sat at the back of his cage and glared," I explained.

"He saw something," Wayne declared. "I know he did."

"I don't want to go there," I pleaded. "You and I didn't see anything. There wasn't anything to see." Still, I couldn't stop the chill that traveled my spine.

"Kiddo, there's a problem down there," he said, soberly. He removed his hands from the equipment grip and faced me. "You got ghosts."

"There's no such thing as spirits or hauntings," Myra said. "I'm sure there's a perfectly good explanation. He saw a spider or something."

"It was somethin' alright," Wayne grumbled. He picked up the sander and trekked out to deposit the machine in my car.

"Thanks, Wayne!" I called.

“It’s probably nothing,” Myra said. She followed Wayne, ran to her SUV, and backed out of the driveway.

I watched Myra and Wayne leave. The porch light flickered, and I shivered.

“Cut it out!” I flipped the switch and locked the door.

CHAPTER 6

I returned the sander at the rental store with a promise I'd be back to rent an edger. Through a downpour, I white-knuckled the drive in heavy city traffic. I parked in the garage, held my breath, and ran through the torrent to the warmth and safety of my townhouse. Wayne's van was absent from the lot, and the lights were off at Mrs. Gilman's unit.

Boots yowled as I burst through the door. His tail up, he weaved between my legs, and nearly tripped me. His earlier trauma was forgotten in his quest for dinner.

Exhausted, I showered and changed into sweats. I rummaged through the fridge for dinner. Slim pickings. I ordered a Hawaiian pizza and gave the delivery guy a generous tip, feeling guilty about dragging him out on a stormy night.

It was heaven biting into the thin crust, cheese, pineapple, and Canadian bacon, and hanging out with Boots, watching television.

Our cozy evening was interrupted by muffled voices coming from the hall. The timber of Wayne's deep voice registered a protest, and Mrs. Gilman's high-pitched tone chimed her response. Her door slammed. Further down, I heard Wayne's door close.

"Doesn't sound good," I commented. Boot's eyes were half closed, sated from his food. "At least they're communicating."

I pondered Wayne's comment about the rehab. "You got ghosts," he'd said.

The house was vacant. The case closed. It was unfortunate the perpetrator had gotten off, but that was the legal system. Skye Jones had paid the ultimate price, and that bothered me. Her diary told of a young woman on the cusp of becoming an adult and discovering men. I didn't know what I could do to avenge her death or put her spirit to rest. If there was a ghost, there was slim evidence of a haunting. Everything could be explained logically.

I contemplated the 'ghostly' happenings. There was Boots' reaction to the basement. But he was a cat. There were the intermittent lights, probably electrical problems. The open window in Skye's room that Myra had insisted she hadn't touched. Wayne must have opened it. Possibly, he opened it for ventilation, a stretch. With a sinking feeling, that was unlikely because he'd been working on the first floor. A trespasser, maybe? It was odd.

Shaking my head. I retreated to the kitchen and deposited my plate in the dishwasher. Grabbing my purse, I dug out Skye's journal. Settling into the sofa, I reread a few passages. She complained of noises in the night, likely Ruston or even Daemon, but she reported hearing a woman crying, weeping. Could there have been another resident? I shrugged, as I read. The noises could have been anything, creaking floorboards, squeaky doors, a stray cat.

Rap, rap, rap!

"Awwk!" I jumped at the knock.

"Hey, Wifey. Are you in there?" Eddy called.

I ran to the door and flung it open. "You've got to quit calling me Wifey!"

"It gets your attention." He grinned.

"But not in a good way," I hissed.

"Sorry." He scanned my sweatshirt and pants get up. His gaze lingered on my hair, and I brushed it from my face.

"What do you want?"

"Dropping off the rent check. Saw your light on." He smiled; his voice soft.

"I'll take the check."

He held it out. I snatched the check and peered at the numbers. "It's for the full amount," I said, pleased.

"Yep, I put in some overtime at work." He smiled.

"Thanks, Eddy. I appreciate it." I could rest easy with the expenses on Hiptown this month. Maybe even get the wiring checked. He shuffled his feet, and looked at the floor.

"Do you want to come in for pizza, a beer?"

"Gee, that'd be great." His face lit up, and I stood aside.

"Pizza is in the kitchen. Help yourself to a brew. I'll be right back." I dashed to the bathroom and brushed and sprayed my hair into something resembling a hairdo.

"So, Eddy. No date tonight?" I asked, getting a lite beer.

"Nope. And you, no date either?" he asked, with a smirk.

"Well, it is Saturday night," I joked. He snickered, his brown eyes sparkled, and the room was quiet while we both sipped our drinks.

He finished the last of a pizza slice, offering a bit to Boots. The cat gobbled it and licked Eddy's fingers. Stretching back on the sofa, he patted his stomach.

"What's that?" He spotted Skye's thin journal.

"It's a diary I found at the Hiptown house. A girl was murdered there."

"Wow. And you're doing the renovation?" His eyes widened.

"Yep," I nodded, resigned that I'd taken on the project.

"What's it say?" He picked up the journal and thumbed through the pages.

"Not a lot. She hears noises, like a girl crying."

"What do you think?" He laid the book on his chest and gazed at me.

"Don't know." I squirmed. I sat opposite his long, lean form. Boots had curled up on the back of the couch.

"Have you heard anything weird?"

"No. Nothing like that," I said hastily, brushing away the memory of the unexplained open window and slamming doors.

His brows furrowed, and he said abruptly, "You should ask the sheriff if he knows anything about the house. Maybe another woman lived there?"

"Hum. That's a good idea." I sipped my drink.

Rap, rap!

"Sounds like you've got more company." He teased with a grin.

"What is this, a party," I muttered as I leapt up and checked the peephole. Don met my gaze through the small opening. *Speak of the devil.*

I opened the door.

"Good evening, Kate."

"Hi?" I stared at him for a moment.

"Sorry to drop by like this. I saw your lights. I thought we might grab a bite to eat."

He saw Eddy's truck in the parking lot.

"I have pizza."

"Can I come in?" His deep blues appraised me. He wore jeans and a brown leather bomber-style jacket. His blond hair was freshly combed, not a hair out of place.

I stepped aside, and motioned him in.

"Hi, Don, we were just talking about you," Eddy said. He remained sprawled on the couch, holding a beer in one hand, waving the book in the other.

"Hey, Eddy. Bad time, Kate?" Don's gaze flicked over my sweats and frizzy hair. Self-conscious, I smoothed my locks.

"No. Help yourself to pizza. There's beer and cola. I'll get changed." I scooted to the bedroom to slip into jeans and a white, cable-knit sweater. A quick glance in the mirror confirmed the worst. My hair had morphed into a wild concoction. Another hair goo failure. I tugged at it furiously, pulling it back in a ponytail. While I futzed with my hair, I heard Eddy's tenor and Don's low, smooth voice in the living room. I emerged from the bedroom to see Eddy, still relaxed, his arm draped around the cat who had hopped down from his perch.

Don sat stiffly in the chair; one knee crossed over the other. He balanced a can of cola on the arm of the chair with one hand, observing Eddy and Boots with a wry smile.

"Katie, I was telling Don about your diary from the rehab," Eddy said. "About how Skye hears someone crying."

"Interesting bit of information. Thought you were going to give me the book, if there was anything new in it." Don's tone was mildly irritated.

"It's her impression." I glared at Eddy. "She doesn't say she *sees* another woman. She thinks she may be dreaming or imagining it. She puts it down to stress. It happens in the middle of the night."

"Let me see."

I took the volume and flipped to the last entry and read:

"I took a knife from the kitchen and hid it under my pillow. He'll be sorry if he tries anything funny. Daemon thinks Ruston was just drunk. He said he would talk to him. The jerk hasn't done anything for a week. I'm losing it. I woke at two in the morning, and I could swear I heard a girl crying. It was far away, like it was downstairs or even the basement. Probably just a dream. I'm really stressed." I handed the journal to Don, the page open to the passage. He took it, scanning the entry.

"She was scared if she armed herself with a knife," Don said. "Could be something. Could be nothing."

"Katie and I thought you might know if there was another tenant?"

I frowned at Eddy. *Why was he talking like we were a couple, asking about my rehab?*

"Don't recall any other resident. I'll check into it," he said, closing the journal and placing it on the coffee table.

"That would be great. I'd appreciate it," I said.

"Sure, Katelyn," Don scanned my expression. He rose, gesturing towards the exit. "I'll go now. Thank you for the soft drink, and the hospitality."

"Did you get some pizza?"

"You know, pineapple on a pizza isn't normal, Katelyn," he said, and chuckled.

Eddy guffawed, sat up, and perched on the edge of the sofa, "Hey, are you driving the Corvette tonight?"

"I am. Do you want to go for a little spin? It's raining, top's up." He shrugged with a little laugh. "Still a fun ride."

"That would be awesome!" Eddy rose from the sofa and grabbed his jacket. "That car is the hottest ride around."

"It's a pretty cool car," Don agreed, grinning.

Speechless, I watched the two men navigate to the exit. Don was out of the gate first.

"Thanks, Kate," Don said.

"Yeah. Thanks, Kate," Eddy chimed and closed the door.

"Thanks, Kate," I mimicked the voices to the closed door. "Men," I said to Boots. He glanced over, licked his paws, and curled into a ball.

CHAPTER 7

I rolled over and groaned when the telephone jangled at seven Sunday morning. It had been a sleepless night. Reviewing the prior evening's events had kept me awake until nearly four a.m. I answered when I saw it was the sheriff.

"Don't you ever sleep?"

"Good morning, Katelyn. I'm sorry if I woke you, but I thought I owed you breakfast or lunch after dropping in last night."

I was quiet for a minute, considering my options.

"Okay, brunch. Pick me up at ten." I hung up and fell back to sleep, then woke again with a start. I looked at the clock and realized the sheriff would be at my door in a half an hour.

I dashed to the kitchen, put on a pot of French roast and headed to the bathroom. I brushed my teeth, washed my face, threw on makeup, and fixed my hair in record time. I ran to the bedroom to get dressed when there was a loud knock. "Dang it!"

Throwing on a robe, I hurried to the door. A glance through the security opening and confirmed it was Don. I threw open the door, saying, "Have some coffee. I'm running late," and dashed back to the bedroom and changed into a sweater and pair of slacks, and emerged to find the sheriff settled into the corner of the sofa, thumbing through Skye's diary. Absently, he reached for the mug while he read. Boots sniffed his pant legs suspiciously. He paused, smiled, and held up his cup. "Great coffee," and sipped.

"Thanks." I watched him warily.

"Uh huh." He kept reading.

"I'll feed Boots."

He cleared his throat. "I suppose you want to know why I'm here."

"You offered food?" My back stiffened, waiting for his response. I got kibble for Boots and put out fresh water. "Or maybe to apologize?"

"True," he conceded. "I wanted more information from the diary."

"Ahh." I poured fresh java from the carafe and joined him in the living room.

"I wanted the dates for Skye's entries. See if anything prompts a memory." He took another gulp of coffee and met my gaze. "Katelyn, you were very hospitable. I should have called. Yes. That's an apology."

"Thank you. Apology accepted."

He cleared his throat, and asked, "You and Eddy have an amicable relationship as exes?" I sat across from him, and cradled my mug.

"Eddy's easy going. He dropped off the rent check."

"Rent check?"

"He rents the Bluebird house. I could not get a buyer, and he needed a place. So, it worked." Being a landlord hadn't been my first choice. It was a win-win solution for both of us. It got him off my couch and he got a sweet rent-to-own deal.

"Ahh."

"You two had a good time?" I asked.

"Yep. That Eddy *is* easy to get along with. I took him for a spin and dropped him off at his house. I'm a stickler for not drinking and driving."

"It was two light beers, maybe. He's a tall guy," I protested.

"It's still drinking." I shifted under his steady gaze and crossed my legs.

"Okay." I shrugged. "Probably within the legal limits." *There I go again, challenging the law.*

"We should go," he said and rose. "How does Joseph's in Hidden Falls sound?"

"Wonderful." I grabbed my handbag and jacket. Joseph's had scrumptious Sunday brunches and a picturesque setting on the St. Croix River. I practically drooled thinking about the food.

Eddy's pickup was in the parking lot when we left my house. *How is he going to get his truck?*

A light rain started as we hurried to his car. Don lifted his arm, opening his bomber jacket to shield my head from the drizzle.

"Sorry, no umbrella."

I rushed to the passenger's side of his jazzy red Corvette. He opened the door and hurried around to the driver's seat.

"This rain seems to go on forever," I said. I buckled up and patted my hair.

"It sure does," and cranked the engine. He grinned as he shifted through the gears and drove to the freeway that led to Hidden Falls.

We were seated in a booth at the restaurant overlooking the jagged terrain of the river town. I ordered a glass of champagne. Don requested a coke. We ambled to the buffet line and filled our plates with pancakes, ham, eggs, and sausage. Then we headed back to our booth and feasted in companionable silence.

"Any room for the dessert bar?" he asked, smiling.

"I'm stuffed." I sat back. "This was awesome."

"It's darned good." He leaned against the back of the leather booth, patting his stomach in agreement, then squinted at me, curious. "Eddy's your ex-husband. But Myra said you are a widow. How is that?"

"Yes. I am widowed." I sipped the champagne and fingered the rim of the glass. "Eddy and I were high school sweethearts, and married young. The marriage lasted a year. After we divorced, I married Jake. We were together for twelve years."

"What happened?"

I sat for a moment, bracing myself. "He jumped in front of a train that was about to run over a young man."

"Wow."

"Wow, is right. Jake thought he could outrun the locomotive. He could not. The young man survived. Jake threw him out of the way, and the train hit him. I usually tell people he died in a car accident. Simpler that way." I shrugged and sipped my drink.

"The train couldn't stop." He gave a low whistle.

"No." I shifted in my seat. "According to the police report, Jake stopped at the railroad crossing for a train. A kid was toting a backpack, wearing earbuds, and loitering on the tracks, lost in his cell phone. The kid didn't hear or see the locomotive coming. Jake jumped out of his car and flung him from the tracks."

"Jake was quite a guy." He paused. "Whew. And the kid was okay?"

"Yes, to both." I nodded and fingered my champagne flute, avoiding the sheriff's eyes. "How about you? Have you been married?" The server laid the bill at the table.

"Nope. Came close once. She died. It was a car accident." He coughed and took a swig of cola. He slipped his wallet from a back pocket, scanned the bill, and laid down a credit card. The server swooped in and took the tab.

"I'm sorry."

"Yeah." He flinched. "It's tough to lose someone." He signed the credit card ticket and slipped the card and receipt into his wallet.

Reaching across the table, he took my hand with his, released it, and stood.

"I'll take you home. I'm doing the second shift today. Need to get some sleep."

"Sure." I scooted from the booth, and we left, hand in hand.

Eddy's truck was gone by the time we made it home. I smiled. *Eddy can take care of himself.*

As Don walked me to the entry, the rain picked up and ratcheted into a steady downpour.

I unlocked my townhouse and turned to him, aware of his closeness. He bent over, held my chin in his hand, and planted a kiss on my lips. He stopped, drew back, our eyes locked, and he kissed me again. Then he left.

His kisses kept me warm and happy, even with gray skies the rest of the day.

CHAPTER 8

I was ready to head to the renovation Monday morning with a plan to rent the edger, to finish sanding the floors. I was still on a high from Sunday brunch with Don when the telephone rang.

"We got a problem, Kiddo." Wayne sounded grim.

The happy feeling evaporated. "What's that?"

"Basement's flooded. There's about three inches of standing water."

"I'll be right there." My stomach churned. I slipped on my jacket, grabbed my purse and bag lunch, and headed out. The sky had cleared, and the rain had quit.

I pulled up to the rehab, and hot-footed it to the house. Wayne met me at the back door.

"How did it happen?" My exasperation added to my gut churn.

"Windows were open. Rain's been pouring in. Maybe since Saturday." His face was pallid.

I thought of the mice disposal he had done on Saturday as we left. As if he read my mind, "I didn't do it. I swear I didn't open no windows. Least of all, when it was raining."

"I believe you." I trekked downstairs and stopped on the bottom step, seeing a small lake.

"It's a mess," Wayne warned, standing behind me.

I tentatively put one foot on the floor. Clear water sloshed over my tennis shoe. "We've got to get this up," I said, panicky.

"Yep." He grimaced.

I stepped with both feet into the water and slogged through the area, my shoes getting soaked. The pool was over my footwear, but not as high as my ankles.

"Great. Just great," I muttered.

"Flood didn't reach the mechanicals, and the washer and dryer aren't connected. They'll dry out."

"Okay. What do we do now?" I asked, defeated. The dismal cellar and the dim storage room mocked me. The windows were shut now. Bits of cobwebs hung along the inside of the casements. The patched section on the cement wall showed more peeling and flaking, a sure sign of poor curing. The added moisture would not help.

"I've got a shop vac in the van, but one or two portable pumps would work best. That should remove all the water. Get a bunch of fans, dry it out."

"What about the mouse traps?"

"I'll get them. You go on to the rental store," he urged.

"Okay." Resigned, still anxious, but with a plan in place, I raced to the equipment leasing store, mulling over who opened the windows. Wayne said he had not left them open. It didn't seem like he'd forget or lie. Then, who did?

I couldn't dwell on it. I had to get the flood up and dry the floor as soon as possible. I did not want to know what kind of mold and bacteria could grow in stagnant water.

At the leasing store, I explained what had happened, and the clerk steered me to utility pumps, hoses, and a dehumidifier. I added a couple of heavy-duty fans. I could muster a fan from Wayne, maybe one from Myra, along with a fan from home. It was a start. Signing the rental agreements, I headed back to the rehab.

Wayne helped haul the equipment downstairs. Stepping through the pool, we hooked the pump to the garden hose, letting the tube drain the water into the laundry tub.

We switched back and forth using the wet vac. When one of us became weary of emptying the wet vacuum, the other operated the machine. It was heavy, nasty work. But we kept at it through the morning, making a dent in the progress. Our energy waning, we took a break on the porch. The day was bright and sunny, a welcome change from the weeks of spring rain. The sun was a ray of hope as we spent our time day baling out the dingy, soaked basement.

"At least the water didn't reach the furnace," I said. I sat on a cast-off wooden chair.

Wayne rested on the half wall that bordered the portico. He tapped out a cigarette from the pack in his shirt pocket, lit it, and inhaled. "Don't know how those windows got open," he said and grimaced.

"Someone had to open them," I said. "It doesn't make sense to open them to air the place out. It's been raining off and on all week." I hesitated, "Could we have forgotten to lock up?" I hated to ask. He had been the last one to leave. It was best to broach it, figure it out, and move on.

"Don't rightly think I did." He sounded hurt.

"I'm sure it wasn't deliberate, stuff happens," I said, hastily. "Can you tell if anything is missing?"

"Didn't see nothing gone."

"If the house was accidentally left unsecured, maybe somebody walked in. Possibly kids, who thought it would be a lark to open them?"

"Didn't leave the door open. You got ghosts. That's a fact."

I wouldn't challenge Wayne further. Somehow, I would find out who opened them. I didn't want to lose his help by pushing his buttons.

"Maybe a vandal jimmied the lock?"

"You know?" he slapped the side of his head. "The back door was open when I got here! Plum forgot with all the excitement. I walked through the kitchen and living room. Didn't see nothing. Went to check the traps in the cellar. That's when all hell broke loose, and I called you."

"The kitchen door was open when you arrived?"

"Yep. Sorry, it just hit me," he said sheepishly and took a puff of his cigarette.

"This door," and I pointed at the front entry, "was locked?"

"Yep. I unlocked it when you brought the pump and fans. Easier to move the machines."

"See? No ghosts, just trespassers." Now, to figure out how to deal with intruders. Maybe locking up had slipped his mind when he left. I wasn't convinced he didn't forget, his mind on autopilot. Distracted, I have locked myself out of my car more than once. I've searched high and low for keys, later finding them in my jeans pocket.

"I'll call a locksmith. After we finish baling out the basement."

"Sounds good."

"How are you and Gillie?" I asked, rising from the chair. Considering, he might have been distracted by Gillie. If he were preoccupied with a disagreement, that could have made him forgetful.

"That woman is impossible," he grumped. He stubbed out his cigarette on the sole of his shoe, stripping the rest of the tobacco, and letting it loose on the lawn. He stood up.

"Oh, oh." I flinched thinking about Saturday night's slamming doors at the townhouse.

"Went out to supper, Saturday. Had a real nice steak dinner." He jabbed his glasses on his bridge. "Then she wants to go home. Says she's tired."

"All right?"

"Doesn't want to stay for dessert. Doesn't ask me in for coffee. Nothing. Just eat and run!" Wayne's jaw jutted out, remembering the night.

"Maybe, she really was fatigued," I offered.

"What's she got to be tired about? There's no gardening yet. What's she doing all day," he ranted. "Something's not right. And she won't talk!"

"I'm sorry, Wayne." I didn't want to add fuel to the fire. When he calmed down, I would tell him about the extended conversations I'd seen her in with the mailman. Then again, maybe I should mind my own business. "She was weary. A little off. She'll come around."

"I s'pose," he said.

"We'd better get back to it," I said. "It'll work out with Gillie." I tried to sound encouraging. I wanted to see him smile.

"Yep, water ain't going to evaporate."

I followed Wayne inside, detouring to study the back entry. It didn't appear someone had tampered with the lock. Still, a little prevention was worth a pound of cure. A new bolt would slow an intruder and offer better security.

I may have to call the police.

We trudged to the cellar. Wayne powered up the vac. I sloshed through the flood to examine the windows. They were an awning style that opened into the basement, likely replacements for the originals. The memory of the man wearing an army-style coat and beanie hat running through the backyard in the rain, flashed. Could someone force the windows in from the outside? Not likely, with the latch in the middle. Unless they were left unlatched.

I tried my theory. I unlatched the window. Wayne's back was to me as he removed water from the dank cellar. I marched upstairs and outside to the windows. Kneeling in front of one, I shoved the sides of the frame. With a squeak, it opened. My heart beat faster, and I sat back on my heels. Possibly someone undid the latches at some point and pushed them open later. Either to gain access to the house or cause mischief. Or, it had been a simple mistake. Except, I could not remember a time when Wayne, Myra, or I would have opened them.

My deliberation was interrupted by a pause in the vac. I hustled to the basement. Wayne emerged from the fruit cellar and emptied the tank. He wiped his brow with his shirtsleeve and returned to the storage room.

I closed the window and locked it. Who had opened them? I had aggravated Wayne enough for one day with my questions. I would not pressure him again. We had a basement to dry out.

He trekked from the storage area again, carrying a full tank. I took the container and emptied it into the laundry tub. We worked in tandem, one running the machine, the other on standby to drain the tank. By early afternoon, with running the portable pump and using the vac, we had removed most of the flood.

"Break time," I said. "Did you bring a lunch?"

"Nope. Out of smokes. I'll grab something at the station." Wayne had a fondness for the hotdogs and brats at the local gas station.

Perspiring and worn out, we headed back upstairs.

"I'll call the locksmith," I said.

He slipped on his jacket. “Can I get you anything?”

“No, thanks. I have a sandwich.” I grabbed my bag with a peanut butter sandwich I had thrown together and refilled my coffee from the thermos in the kitchen.

“I’ll be back.”

“I’ll be on the porch.” I snagged my cell phone. Easing into the chair, I scarfed my sandwich in record time. Then I closed my eyes and leaned back, thinking about my next move. I had rented the equipment for a day and hadn’t plugged in the dehumidifier or used the fans. I could keep everything until tomorrow morning. No need to rush. Removing the flood made me feel better about the calamity.

I Googled locksmiths and called Fast Freddie’s Locksmith. He was nearby and said he could re-key the doors for about a hundred dollars and be there within the hour. I gritted my teeth and agreed. It would provide peace of mind. Even if his business name gave me pause.

I dialed Myra while I waited.

“What’s new?” I asked in a sober voice.

“What’s going on?”

“The basement at Hiptown flooded over the weekend.”

“Oh, no! Did a pipe break?” she asked.

“No broken pipe. Thanks for planting the idea.” *I’ll have to have any exposed water pipes or connections inspected.* “The cellar windows were wide open.”

“What? It has been raining for weeks. Why would the windows be open?”

“Good question. I think somebody entered and pulled a prank. Or, they were open at one point, and not locked.” I paused, and added, “Wayne said the back door was unlatched when he arrived this morning.”

“Vandalism. People don’t have enough to do,” she said firmly.

“Do you think I need to call the police?”

"You should report it."

"Okay." Sensing my hesitation. "Did something happen with Sheriff Don?"

Drat Myra. I swear she could read my mind.

"No. He wouldn't take calls here, anyway," I answered quickly, remembering Don's parting kiss. "There's nothing gone. And, I hate to get the cops involved if it was just a silly mistake."

"You think Wayne opened them?" she asked, with a note of disbelief.

"He's been preoccupied by some problems with Gillie. He doesn't think he left the door unsecured. But I've done things automatically. It may have been a mistake."

"Have you checked around outside? Could anyone get in from outdoors?"

"It's possible if they were unlocked," I conceded. "Gotta go, the locksmith is here. Oh, do you have an extra fan?"

"I'll check."

"If you do, would you drop it off? I could use one more."

"Will do," she said.

I signed off from Myra and watched a Fast Freddie company van stop at the house.

A short, wiry man leaped out of the driver's side and strode to the vestibule. One leg dragged slightly, and he had a slight hop as he walked. He wore a navy work jacket, jeans, and a ball cap with the logo of his company.

I met him at the sidewalk.

"Hey, there. You the lady who called for the locksmith?" he asked, a huge smile showing deep dimples.

"I am. You're Fast Freddie?" Taking in his big smile and brown eyes magnified by plastic brown-rimmed glasses. I guessed him to be in his thirties, maybe younger, because of his engaging manner.

"Fast Freddie, I am," he said. He lifted his hat from his longish, brown hair and asked, "You the owner?"

"I am."

"This the lock?" and he nodded toward the front entry.

"Yes. And the back door too," I said.

"How many keys?"

"Four should do it." I figured one for me, Wayne, Myra, and a spare.

"Hey, yeah. Costs extra for four keys." He grinned.

"Of course." *Everything is extra.* Mentally, I tallied the cost of the leased equipment against my budget for rehabbing the home. Thank goodness for the cushion left from the last rehab. The job happened courtesy of Myra's brother, the police chief who used his connections to get a contract for Ariel's unit in my townhouse complex. After Ariel was murdered, Myra had called her brother, who had called the family, who had called their lawyer. The lawyer convinced the family to renovate Ariel's unit and recommended me for the job. It had been a sweet deal.

While Fast Freddie worked, I trotted around back to check the lower windows. On my knees, I inspected the ground and casings. There wasn't much to see. If there had been any activity outside, the rain had washed it away.

I brushed off my jeans and headed to the front entry where Fast Freddie was trying a new key.

"Here, try it." He motioned toward the lock. I slipped in the key, locking and unlocking it.

"Have you changed the other door?"

"Hey, not yet. I'll get it." He smiled and nodded.

"Sure."

I trekked to my car for the fans and dehumidifier while Freddie hopped to the back exit and changed the lock. After depositing the machines in the cellar, I waited for Freddie on the porch with a fresh cup of coffee.

"Hey, lady. Your locks are done." Freddie appeared on the sidewalk. He adjusted his hat, scratched his forehead, and grinned.

"Great." I set my mug on the half wall and ambled to the back. Fast Freddie limped behind me.

He watched me try the keys.

"Hey, why are you changing the locks?"

"Looks like we have a vandal. Someone got in last weekend and opened the cellar windows; it flooded," I said, with a sigh.

"Hey, that's tough." He steadied himself, adjusting his bum leg. "Hey, could be a ghost? Folks in this neighborhood believe the place is haunted."

"Not you, too," I groaned. I twisted the key and stared at Fast Freddie. "You've lived in this area for a while?"

"Sure have." He broke away from my stare, and said, "Hey, a girl was killed here. Found her buried over there," and he gestured to the ground next to the garage.

"I heard about that," I said grimly. "I doubt a ghost would have the dexterity to open windows."

"Yeah." He nodded. "People talk. Could be somebody with a spare key," he quipped. "Good thing you're getting new locks." And he gave me another huge, dimpled smile.

I regarded him quizzically. I had had two keys made, with the two I had received at closing. I had the copies made when I bought the house. Myra and Wayne each had one, I carried one, with the spare stashed at home.

"Hey. Happens all the time. People give out keys or hide a spare and forget. It keeps Fast Freddie in business." His owl-like eyes sparkled, and he grinned.

Dang. Maybe there are other keys out there.

I paid Fast Freddie and called the police to report suspected vandalism.

CHAPTER 9

The officer who took the report was a thirty-something, solidly built, friendly woman, with short brown hair. I breathed easy that Don would not be in on the call. The Hiptown rehab was out of his territory.

The woman appeared sympathetic about the flooded basement. She checked the cellar windows, inside and out. She checked doors and didn't find any sign of forced entry. Taking notes, she said there was little she could do. Nothing had been stolen, and there wasn't any sign that someone had entered and opened the windows before, or during, the rainstorm. It was only my suspicion that there had been a trespasser.

"There will be a record of suspected vandalism if anything more happens here. It's smart to change the locks."

"Thank you. I didn't know if I should report it," I added. "The door may have been left open by mistake."

Wayne drove up while the officer and I spoke.

"Found the back door open when I got here this morning. Just forgot it when I found the danged basement flooded," he explained, his gray ponytail flipping as he talked.

"Sure. Understandable." The officer nodded. "This is a busy area, with lots going on."

Hiptown was a magnet for young and old alike. It had edgy shops, coffeehouses, and was home to many students. It was a major transit area for buses traveling to the university and downtown Minneapolis. Homeowners enjoyed the lakes and proximity to stores, with a shopping center within two blocks.

After the police officer drove away, Wayne and I headed back to work. I was preoccupied with the day's events. *Wayne forgot the door was open when he arrived early that morning. He's been a little off since he and Gillie had been arguing, and he is uneasy by the ghost rumors.*

I unplugged and removed the portable pump and used the wet vacuum to pull up the remaining water.

"Ready for the dehumidifier and fans," I called, shutting down the vac. I straightened, stretching my back muscles. Wayne emptied the last tank of water and wrapped the cords and the drainage hose preparing to move the equipment.

"I'll take this to the car," he said, grabbing the pump and heading upstairs. I rubbed my shoulders and viewed the progress we'd made drying out the basement. He reappeared with the dehumidifier.

"Looks good." He plugged in the machine.

"Couldn't have done it without you. Thanks, Wayne." The area was nearly back to normal. I breathed a sigh of relief.

"No problem. I'll get the fans."

"I'll go with you." I followed him up the steps to retrieve the fans from the living room. I toted one, and he carried another.

"We're running out of outlets," he said, plugging in a fan.

"After I return the pump, I'll pick up a power strip. If I leave now, I can make the rental store before it closes."

"Sounds good. I'll be here." He trailed me upstairs and out to the porch. He sat on the half wall and gave a thumbs up as I drove off.

My shoulders and back ached, but I was calmer on my way to the rental shop. All and all, I was pleased with our progress. I left the pump with an agreement to return the rest of the equipment in two days. I figured after a couple of days, I could use the fans I had on hand, and avoid more rental fees.

"No problem," the young male clerk said, smiling. "You're a regular."

"Uh huh." I could imagine what I looked like. My sweatshirt felt sticky and my hair stuck to my head with sweat. I hadn't checked my appearance all day, and it wasn't likely I'd see a mirror anytime soon.

I spotted a shiny, red Corvette on the busy street in front of the rental store and my stomach lurched. I ducked and feigned window shopping. I did not want to be seen if the driver was the sheriff enjoying the first sunny day in his jazzy ride. My reflection in the window confirmed it was a solid move. I smoothed my locks and got in the driver's seat. Inside, I combed my hair, glad to have avoided the Corvette.

I drove to the hardware store and picked up two extension cords and a heavy-duty power strip. I hurried to the house. Seeing the sporty vehicle had unnerved me. I shrugged it off. The wet basement was a priority.

Parking in front, I got out, grabbing the bag with the cables and power strip. Wayne navigated to the portico. He took a quick puff of his cigarette as I strode the sidewalk.

"Record time." He grinned, put out his smoke, and rose. I opened the shopping bag. "Kiddo, that'll work. We can do this!"

Myra arrived while we were examining the supplies.

"Hello. I brought a fan. How is it going?" She joined us on the porch, carrying a floor fan.

"Better," I said. "Good timing. We're setting up the fans."

"Yep. All the water's up," Wayne added.

As daylight faded, the three of us headed inside to the cellar with Wayne leading the way.

"You reported the windows were open?" Myra asked, standing on the bottom step, scrutinizing the narrow windows.

"Yep," I said grimly. "Not much they can do. Take the report, keep it on file if anything else happens." I shrugged. "Had the locks changed."

She offered the tall fan to Wayne, and he placed it on the floor next to the washer. Plugging in the strip, he added two fans to the strip. The dehumidifier was on a single outlet.

He connected an extension cord to each fan and put them in different areas. He started one, when he switched on the second fan, the lights blinked and flickered off. The fans quit circulating air.

"Dang it," Wayne cursed. In the dark, he took out his cigarette lighter and lit the way to the breaker and threw the switch. The lights came on and fans started up.

Hisssssss! The breaker box spewed a horrific sizzling sound, the fans stopped, and the cellar was black.

"Oh!" I exclaimed.

Myra gasped.

"What was that?" I asked, alarmed.

In the darkness, I heard Wayne rifle through a pocket and click his lighter. In the hazy glow, he peered at the electrical panel.

"Main's off," he announced. "I ain't touching that. Time to call an electrician."

"Let's get out of here," Myra said. Her breath coming in spurts, she clattered up the stairs. I followed Myra and Wayne followed on my heels, breathing heavily. He held up his lighter to illuminate the steps.

The house was black as we hustled out of the cellar to the front porch. Streetlights gave a hazy light in the dark night.

"Wayne, do you think it will be okay to wait until tomorrow for an electrician?" I'd considered what after hour charges might be.

"Should be okay. The main breaker's off. You and Myra wait here. I'll check and see if I can spot, or smell anything."

"Thanks, Wayne." He entered the house, lighter in hand.

"This is another fine mess I've gotten myself into," I said, and groaned.

"It's an older home. We overloaded the circuits with the machines. The circuit breaker did what it's designed to do, shut off the power," she said, her voice quaked.

"What about the noise from hell?" I asked.

"It was a little spooky." She gave a giggle. Her snicker was contagious, and I chuckled, the sound of my laughter colored with hysteria. By the time Wayne returned to the porch, we had dissolved into gales of laughter. I wiped moisture from my eyes.

"What's so funny," he demanded. "We could have been fried!" He held the light above his head. That sent Myra and me into another burst of helpless giggles. He regarded us soberly, the light from the cigarette lighter casting shadows over his face. He flicked it off, snorted, and laughed.

"It's just been a very long day," I gasped, wiping tears from my cheeks. Struggling to compose myself, I nervously chuckled.

"Yes, it has," Myra agreed, and wiped away a tear of laughter. "We should do Popov's."

"Thanks, Myra. I have to go home and get cleaned up, and find an electrician," I said. "Can't get anything done while the electricity is out."

"No thanks. I'm due at Gillie's."

"Good deal," I said, and smiled.

"Yep. We will see. She called. Wants to talk." He slipped the lighter in his jean jacket pocket.

"Oh." I said, my stomach queasy, "Over dinner, I hope?"

"Yeah. She said she'd have supper for us," and flipped up the hood on his hoodie, avoiding our gazes.

"Well," Myra said, and noted my expression. She shrugged. "Another time."

"Thanks. I'll keep you posted," I said to Myra. "Wayne, I'll see you tomorrow."

"See you, Kiddo." He nodded.

"All right," Myra said. She went to her SUV, Wayne trailed her, and I hiked to my car.

I started the vehicle and sat for a minute studying the house. I hope I hadn't bitten off more than I could chew with this rehab. An electrician was going to be expensive. But I couldn't avoid it any longer. At least, getting the electrical fixed would eliminate the quirky and annoying flickering lights while we worked. It might settle Wayne down and stop his insistence that there was a spirit inhabiting the dwelling.

I pulled away from the curb and headed home, wondering what else could go wrong with this house renovation. I made a detour through the drive-through at Burger World and ate my burger and fries on the way.

Boots scolded me when I dragged in. He could smell the burger. I dropped my bag and coat at the kitchen table and dug out a treat from the treat jar. While he nibbled, I filled his bowl with kibble, and headed to the bathroom, stripping off dirty clothes on the way.

Refreshed from the shower and donning clean sweats, I powered up the computer and settled in to locate an electrician for the next day.

Dynamic Electric won with a 4.7 out of five-star rating, a thirty-dollar coupon, twenty-four-hour service, repairs guaranteed. I made the appointment for nine a.m. the next morning. They wouldn't give an estimate until they saw the job. Naturally.

Fast Freddie's comment about other keys being out there and the rumor the house was haunted bugged me. After I Googled Dynamic Electric, I studied Fast Freddie's Locksmith listing again to see if there was something I missed when I chose him. Hindsight is always twenty-twenty.

It would be convenient for a locksmith to gain entry to a home without raising suspicion among residents. The web identified Fast Freddie's Locksmith, LLC as a privately-owned company, licensed, bonded, and insured with an 'A' Better Business rating. There wasn't an owner's name, but he had answered to Fast Freddie. His dimpled, wide smile, easy manner, and limp convinced me he was harmless.

"Katelyn Baxter, you're tired and paranoid. This business about ghosts is getting to you," I muttered and powered down the computer. Yawning, I tumbled into bed, my body aching from the labor I had done that day.

CHAPTER 10

The next morning, I waited on the porch for Dan from Dynamic Electric. He was punctual. The tall, thin, gray-haired, fifty-something man had a trim mustache and wore silver-rimmed glasses. He wore blue work pants with a blue jacket, decorated with the image of a jagged, red, electric bolt, matching the logo on his truck. He listened to my account of the blinking lights, the fans, and the hissing noise the circuit breaker made when it shut down.

Then, he took a heavy-duty flashlight from his truck and started by verifying the main switch was off, and disconnected the fans and the dehumidifier from the outlets.

"Had some water damage here?" he asked, sniffing the damp air. The standing water had been removed from the floor, but the cement and wooden studs held moisture.

"Yeah," I said. "Windows were open. I think it was vandalism."

"You don't say?" He observed the windows, moving his flashlight along the wall. "There's a streak. There," he said, holding the light still.

I scanned the wall for the mark, stopped and stared. It was easy to miss the smear on the lower portion of the surface. The officer who took the report had viewed the flooded area from the stairs and hadn't seen the mark. The windows were closed, with no evidence of forced entry.

"Someone on the outside could have pushed in the window and entered," Dan suggested. "Had to have been a skinny person."

"Maybe. Didn't see anything outside. Windows latch from inside," I said and rubbed at the brown smudge. "It isn't fresh," I frowned. "It is an old house."

"Then, whoever it was must have entered upstairs," he commented. "Nasty business this water stuff. You want to get this dried out."

"Just as soon as we have electricity."

He examined the outlets, and removed switch plates, checking the wiring behind each receptacle. Methodically, he trekked from the basement to the main level, and to the second floor. Inwardly, I cringed, calculating how much this would cost. When he finished, he flipped on the main. Blessedly, the lights stayed on. He plugged in two fans and the dehumidifier. Everything worked.

"Wiring was slack behind three outlets. Fixed that. Can't overload the circuits. Might have to run extension cords from the main floor to the fans."

"Would a loose wire make the lights go off and on?"

"Yes. A brisk wind can blow around the outdoor wires. If the wiring is not secure, that could make the lights flicker," he said.

"What about the weird hissing noise?"

"Circuit panel did what it's supposed to do, shut down the circuit."

I'd heard that one before.

We migrated to the front porch. Dan disappeared to his vehicle and came back with his bill. I paid him with a credit card, grumbling under my breath, as he handed me the receipt.

"Good luck drying out the basement," he said and drove away.

"No ghosts. Just wonky wiring," I reported to Wayne. He had started the demo on the first-floor master bathroom while Dan inspected the electrical.

"Kiddo, the place still feels creepy." He grunted and pried tile from between the sink basin and medicine cabinet.

It was late afternoon, and daylight was fading fast. Artificial light magnified the gloomy atmosphere of the house under renovation. The walls were unfinished in the new open concept living area. Construction dust covered window ledges, clung to fixtures and baseboards, and floated through the air.

I tapped him on the shoulder.

"Wayne, I need to run two long, heavy-duty extension cords to the basement and connect the fans."

"Got a couple in my van." He laid the pry bar across the sink, took out a handkerchief and wiped his brow. "I'll get 'em."

"That'd be great."

While he was gone, I studied the bathroom, considering what I would do with the dated fixtures. There was a vintage, free-standing, claw-foot tub that would stay. Most buyers in this young neighborhood would want a shower. I had seen a few bathtubs in the older neighborhood's housing stock with custom rods that held a shower curtain. It wasn't the best option, but there wasn't enough space to add a separate shower stall.

Maybe Wayne could enclose the tub. If anyone could do a first-rate job, he would. We'd talk after he completed removing the old tile.

The toilet was functional, albeit rusty from iron stains. I would replace the fixture with one that used less water. The porcelain cover was cracked. Now was as good a time as any to take a closer peek. I wiped the tank top and gingerly removed it. I peered inside. The inside was murky with crud. I cringed and started to replace the porcelain lid. About to position the cover, a piece of tape caught my eye. I hesitated and placed the lid on the floor. Kneeling, I turned it over. A small manila envelope encased in a plastic baggie was fastened with silver-colored duct tape to the underside of the cover.

"What is this?" I frowned and lifted a corner of the tape.

Wayne showed up with the heavy-duty electrical cords.

"Watcha got there?" He put the cords down and watched as I ripped the tape that left a gooey residue on the porcelain.

"Don't know," I said and grimaced. I tugged at the adhesive.

Bammm!

We jumped. I let go of the strip and gasped. "What was that?"

"Sounded like a door," Wayne said. "Slamming."

"Jeepers?" I stared up at him.

Nervously, we looked at each other. He flipped his ponytail; his jaw tight. "I'll check," he said, in a low voice.

"Wait, a second. I'll go with you," I whispered and peeled off the remaining duct tape and slipped the envelope from the baggie, tossing the plastic and tape into the wheelbarrow. Quivering, I tore into the envelope. A photograph fell out. I glanced at it, my heart thumping. I held up the photo.

"Who is this," I gasped. He leaned over and studied the picture.

It was a photograph taken with an old-style, instant Polaroid camera of a young teenager, possibly Native American, wearing blue teardrop earrings. She appeared wide-eyed and innocent at the photographer. Her brown hair was long and parted in the middle.

We heard another creak and a loud bam. My stomach dipped, and heart raced. I stuffed the photo back and rose. Envelope in hand, I started toward the stairs. Wayne armed with the crowbar, placed his hand on my shoulder, stopped me, and stepped in front, leading the way. Anxiously, I shadowed him up the staircase. We stopped on the second-level landing.

The door to Skye's former room was closed. The bathroom door was ajar, as was the entry to Daemon's old room. With the pry bar held high, Wayne strode to the closed door and turned the knob. I stood behind him, holding my breath as he flipped the light switch. I peered around his body into the room. He exhaled, and his shoulders slumped.

"Dang it!" he said, resigned. "Window's open."

"But how?" I asked. I let out a slow breath. *I had not been with the electrician every step of the way. Maybe he got warm and opened the window while he worked.*

"Keep telling ya. Ya got ghosts," he grumbled, and left the tool on the floor. He lowered the sash and twisted the lock on the casing. He cut the switch, and we took one last glimpse of the room. It was nearly dark outside. The low light cast shadows on the walls; he shut the door.

"Let's get out of here," I said. I had had enough.

We scrambled from the house. Wayne, his face grim, locked the front exit.

"Tomorrow?" he asked, turning to me. His face was gray, and his chin set.

"Yes." I nodded. He left; his shoulders squared.

I'd taken just enough time to grab my jacket and handbag, stashing the envelope in my bag. I felt as though my nerves were dancing on top of my skin, and my head ached. In my car, I took a minute and called Myra on my cell. “Are you up for Popov’s?”

She heard the panic in my voice. “When?”

“An hour?”

“I’ll meet you there.”

Relieved, I drove home, cleaned up, and headed out.

Myra was seated in a booth when I joined her at the restaurant. When she saw my expression, she ordered two chardonnays. When the server returned with our wine, I clutched the glass and ordered the works, Popov’s burgers and fries. I leaned back and took a gulp after the server scurried away with our orders.

“What happened?” She sipped her wine and waited.

I dug out the envelope, plucked out the picture and laid it on the table.

“What’s this?” Frowning, she slipped on designer readers and examined the photo.

“I found it in this,” I said, gesturing towards the envelope, “taped under the tank cover in Ruston Ahoe’s old bath.”

“Someone hid it,” she remarked. Studying the image, she added, “Pretty girl.” Her eyebrows raised as she scanned the picture.

“What do you think it means?”

“It’s hard to tell. It may be an old flame, a girlfriend. Might not belong to Ruston at all.” She met my gaze.

“Who else? The house has been vacant since the bank took it back.”

“True.” She frowned. “You should ask the sheriff. It resembles a photo you might see of missing children. It must have been taken a few years back. No one uses instant cameras any longer.” She considered the picture, commenting, “She’s young.”

"I'm thinking fourteen, fifteen. Ruston would be quite a bit older," I mused, reaching for my glass.

"Someone else could have put it there. Another occupant?" she asked, her head tilted, speculating.

"That would leave Daemon Pleasant."

"He was the other tenant," she said. "A visitor might have hidden it?"

"Someone visits Ruston, Daemon, or Skye and asks to use the bathroom and hides a photo under the toilet lid?" I asked, skeptical.

"It's an excellent hiding place." She laughed. "How often do you look under your tank cover?"

"Never," I chuckled.

"There you go." She put the polaroid aside. The cranky brunette was now on duty and delivered our food.

"I get you check," she snapped in broken English and stalked off.

Myra and I did an eye-roll after the server left. Then we dug in, each of us preoccupied with the picture while we ate. Stuffed, I sat back and said, "I think you're right. I will ask Don if he can check missing person records. See if any girls match the photo." I examined the image, perplexed.

"Maybe we'll find out who she is and if she's missing. It could be someone's love interest," she speculated.

"Could be," I nodded. "I'm just very aware of the home's history."

"I understand." She nodded.

"Wayne still thinks the house is haunted." I raised the subject tentatively.

"Oh, no," she groaned, hand rubbing her temple. "Why?"

"Well, the window keeps opening by itself," I said. I sipped wine, avoiding her stare.

She assessed me, wary.

"Well, it's true." I was on the defensive and set my glass down, meeting her stare. "Look at all the trouble we've had with the open windows? No one admits to it. And the lights?"

Wayne's insistence that the rehab was haunted, and a spirit was causing the windows to raise, and doors to slam, was getting to me.

"What did the electrician say about the lights?" she asked, cautiously.

"He said there were a couple of loose wires, plus we overloaded the circuits. The wind, along with the slack wiring, caused the lights to flicker."

"See, that makes perfect sense."

"And the windows," I countered.

"You said you thought it was vandals. You had the locks changed," she chided.

"Yes. But..."

"But, what?"

I met Myra's stare. "It was when I found the photograph, Skye's door slammed. When we investigated, the window was open, again."

"But the electrician could have opened it during his visit?"

"I thought of that. I don't know why he would, but say he did, what about Boots and how he acted in the cellar?"

"He wouldn't come out of his cage, and he yowled? He had a hissy fit?"

"It was more than that. He was staring at something. Something neither of us saw."

"I suppose now you will say Boots saw a ghost?"

"Maybe." I drank the last of my chardonnay.

"You know what I think of ghosts and cleansings," she said, groaning. "Let's not go there." Myra had reluctantly taken part in two sage burning rituals to cleanse my last renovations. The house on Bluebird

Street in Crocus Heights, and my neighbor Ariel's, former townhouse. She was not a fan. She was practical, and believed there was a logical reason behind everything. Me, I'm not so sure.

"It worked, didn't it?" I met her gaze.

"I suppose." She conceded and sighed.

"Eddy seems content in the home. Ariel's house is waiting for the right occupant. Keep an open mind," I pleaded. "I might be in deep doodoo. There have been plenty of strange goings-on and unexpected repairs."

"It will be fine. First, ask the electrician if he opened the window. And show the picture to the sheriff. See if anything rings a bell. If you copy it, I'll send it to my brother."

"I'll do that. But if the electrician says he didn't open it?" I raised my eyebrows.

"First things first," she said, grumbling. She grabbed her handbag beside her on the seat of the booth.

"Right." I smiled, smugly. I would check with the electrician, and ask Don about the photo.

But more and more, it appeared as if a spirit had to be banished from the Hiptown house. I was determined to stop the mysterious happenings in my rehab so I could sell it.

Myra would come around.

CHAPTER 11

The next morning, I left a message for Dan from Dynamic Electric to call me. I left the house armed with foam earplugs, rubber gloves, an old toss pillow, Borax, bleach, and white vinegar. I would wipe down any surfaces that could hold mildew in the cellar.

When I arrived at the rehab, Wayne was already working. He nodded towards me, crowbar in hand, and continued to demo the bathroom. He'd already run the electrical cords from the main floor to the basement to connect the fans. I trekked to the cellar, loaded with supplies and a bucket, avoiding the snaking cords. He'd started the dehumidifier on one outlet and plugged a fan into another to avoid overloading the circuits. It was noisy, and the area sounded like a cacophony of beating drums.

I surveyed the dim area and considered my plan to sanitize the expanse. It was still a creepy, crawly basement. I did not want to add mold to the creep factor. Borax should do the trick. I headed upstairs to fill my coffee mug, get containers for vinegar, and check in with Wayne.

"Wayne." I waved from the entry to get his attention.

"Hey." He put down his pry tool and wiped his hands on his jeans, his long gray hair in his usual ponytail. Nervously, he tugged the hair over his back.

"Are you okay?" He appeared down in the dumps. He rubbed his jaw and swallowed.

"Nope."

"What is it?" I held my breath. *I hope he isn't going to quit.*

"It's Gillie," he blurted.

"Let's take a break," I motioned towards the porch. I breathed a sigh of relief and grabbed my mug. He tapped out a Camel unfiltered cigarette and lit up.

"What happened?" I asked, settling in on the chair.

"Last night, we had supper at her place." He paused. "She said she wanted space."

"Oh," I said, watching him take a drag. "What about you? How do you feel?"

"I'm too old to want 'space!' What the heck is that? I know I'm not perfect. I think there's something going on with that mailman."

"Oh." I thought guiltily about the times I had seen the mail carrier and Mrs. Gilman chatting at the truck.

"You know that saying, 'If you love someone, let them go. If they come back to you, they're yours?' Maybe that's what you need to do with Mrs. Gilman," I said, carefully.

"Yeah. Well, I got another saying, 'If you love someone, let 'em go. If they don't come back to you, hunt 'em down, kill 'em!'" He stubbed his cigarette out on the cement, stripped the remaining tobacco and tossed it on the lawn.

I burst out laughing. "You can't be serious!"

"Naw, I won't kill nobody." He chuckled. "Gonna to talk to Gillie, again. Get to the bottom of this 'space' stuff. Huh!" He snorted.

"Maybe you should. It would clear your mind, anyway."

"Yep. That's what I'm gonna do." He stood and headed inside. "Good talk," he said, as he cleared the door.

"Glad to help." I followed. With renewed vigor, he resumed demolishing the bathroom.

I rummaged through the kitchen, found an old jar and an empty coffee tin. I tucked the vessel under my upper arm and grabbed the can with the same hand. With my free hand, I gripped my cup and headed back to work. I poured white vinegar into the two containers and found spots for them. White vinegar would clear the dank air. I poured a cup of borax into a gallon of hot water. I put in earplugs to stem the racket from the fans and dehumidifier and slipped on rubber gloves. Using the pillow to cushion my knees, I scrubbed the wood and worked my way around the basement perimeter, stopping when I reached the doorway to the old canning storage room.

I stood and scanned the area. There was a ledge where food would have been stored. Amid the cobwebs, a newer block of cement served as a wall and bordered the stairwell. The cement surface was peeling. The wall must have failed at some point, and someone tried to stabilize the area with new concrete. I grabbed the broom and swiped at the cobwebs. I stopped sweeping and hesitated. Listening, I thought I heard the muffled sound of an animal, maybe a cat, through the earplugs. Shaking, I felt a chill. I removed the earplugs and stuffed them in my pants pockets. I stilled myself and strained to hear. Nothing, except the sounds of the equipment.

I shook myself and glanced at the floor. Wayne's grumbling about the house being haunted was getting to me. I would wait on applying the borax solution in the small room. Instead, I aimed the dehumidifier into the space.

I had picked up a moisture meter on my earlier shopping trip for the cleaning supplies. The gizmo measured the level of dampness in wood. I circled the basement's central area and tested the moisture levels in the studs. It was drying nicely. I would keep the dehumidifier until the day's end and return it the next day with the rental fans. We could work with the fans Wayne, Myra, and I supplied and cut back on the equipment rental bill.

I considered Myra's suggestion to ask the sheriff about the photo, see if it rang any bells. I did not want a lecture that I should have called right away if I found anything suspicious in the house.

The memory of Don's warm kiss tugged at the back of my mind, and I hesitated calling. I hadn't heard anything from him in a couple of days. If he was interested, he would call.

I didn't know what to make of the photo of the girl. The picture had been stashed, and that troubled me. Who was she, and what did the picture mean?

I considered the possibility Don would have access to missing person records. It couldn't hurt to ask if he would check it out. I would put aside my reluctance to get more information about the girl.

"Wayne, I'm heading home for lunch," I called.

"I'll head over to the station for a hotdog," he said, with a grin. He was still demolishing the first-floor master bath.

I stopped short of the door. "You didn't hear a cat, did you?"

"Nope." He shook his head and shot me a knowing look. "You heard it, too?"

"I'm sure it was nothing." I grimaced. I had just given him more ammunition to his claim the house was haunted.

Getting through the city at noontime was a bear. I was stopped at every red light and impatiently waited for the signals to change. Now that I had decided to call Don, I was in a hurry to get the mission accomplished.

At home, I powered up the printer. I made two copies of the picture, one for Myra's brother, the police chief, and one for Don. I took a few minutes to Google "hauntings" and remedies, remembering Wayne's expression when I asked about the noise.

After scarfing a peanut butter sandwich, tossing a treat to Boots, and recalling Don's kiss, I dialed.

"Katelyn. What a pleasant surprise." He answered on the first ring. I loved and hated Caller ID.

"Hi, Don, er Sheriff." *This was business.*

"Don," he said firmly. "To what do I owe the pleasure of your call?" His voice was low and warm, and I felt my face go beet red as I babbled.

"I have a picture I'd like you to see."

"A picture?" He paused. "What kind of picture?"

"It's of a young girl. I found it taped to the underside of the tank cover in what was Ruston Ahoe's master bath. Wayne started rehabbing the room yesterday."

"Okay." Silence.

I cleared my throat. "It may be nothing. But, because the picture was hidden, makes me wonder if it means something. Myra thought it would be good to run it past you." I threw in her name to make my call sound legitimate, and I wasn't using a lame excuse. She would be okay with my dropping her name.

"I want to see it," he said, abruptly. "When can we make that happen?"

"I'm at home now and will head back to the Hiptown house after lunch."

"I'll meet you there," he said, crisply and hung up.

I frowned at the receiver. "Could have said goodbye, or something," I grumbled. I disconnected, checked the time, and hustled to the bathroom. My hair was wild, and I wore no make-up. I was dressed in my worst set of grungy work clothes. That wouldn't do. I changed into a better pair of jeans, a clean sweatshirt, threw on makeup, and worked the curling iron, trying to tame my wild tangle of curls. I sprayed my hair with everything I had and stood back. "Better," I said to Boots, who'd sat on his haunches on the bathroom rug the entire time, observing my flurry of activity. He wrinkled his nose, licked his paws, and stalked away.

"Little help here," I called to the cat.

I hurried to the kitchen table/desk and stuffed the copies and original photo back in the manila envelope. I shoved the packet into my bag, grabbed my jacket, and left for the rehab.

When I arrived in front of the house about a half an hour later, a squad car was parked in the driveway behind Wayne's van. Wayne stood on the portico, bending Don's ear. He gestured widely, grimacing as he talked, his ponytail flipping. My guess was that he was recounting the problems with the renovation.

I got out of my car and approached cautiously. My belief was confirmed when I heard his voice boom, "The lights kept going off and on. And then the danged basement flooded!"

Coming in at the end of his tirade, I said, "Wayne's been a brick through all the troubles with the project."

"Thanks, Kiddo. But there ain't nothing I can do to fix a haunted house!"

The sheriff gave me a cool side wise glance that said, "cuckoo bird" and turned his attention back to Wayne. With a slight smile, he said, "You've put in a lot of long hours."

"He has," I agreed. "Wayne, take the rest of the day off. I have more cleaning to do in the cellar. It might be a marvelous time to call Gillie. You said you wanted to talk some things out. Or, take in a movie, do something fun."

"You sure you want to be here alone?" He observed me with narrowed eyes, his expression serious.

"I'll call Myra. She'll keep me company."

"Okay," he conceded. "Might be good to get away."

"I'm sure of it."

Wayne glanced from me to the sheriff, winked. "Be back tomorrow morning."

"Sounds good."

"I'll move my car," Don said. He backed out and parked on the street behind my car.

Wayne collected his coat from the house, slipping a jean jacket over his hoodie. "Now, you promise you're gonna call Myra?" he asked. "Cuz I don't think it's safe for you to work here alone, with all the goings-on."

"I will. I'll be fine." I nodded. "You have fun."

"Thanks!" He walked to his van. His hand on the door handle, he stopped, turned, and paused, expectantly.

I took out my cell and dialed. When Myra answered, "Got a favor. Wayne's off for the day. Can you come to the renovation and keep me company? The sheriff's here now, but he'll be leaving soon."

"I'm on my way." She hung up, and I waved at Wayne, and yelled, "She's coming."

"I'll wait until she gets here," Don shouted. We watched him drive away.

"Wrapped a little tight," he said, smiling.

"He's a little protective. This house renovation has been tough, and he has problems with Gillie."

"Woman problems?" He grinned. "I can imagine."

My face burned, and I gestured towards the entry. "I'll show you what I found." Inside, I dug out the envelope containing the picture from my purse.

"This is a copy?"

"Yes."

"May I have the original?"

"Sure." I took back the copy and fished out the Polaroid.

"Is that the envelope you found the picture in?" He eyed the faded container.

"Yes."

"I'd like that, too."

"Okay." I removed the second copy, and handed him the wrapper, stuffing the two copies in my handbag, I placed the bag in a corner of the vestibule.

He studied the image.

"Where did you find this?" His deep blues met my stare.

"In here." I pointed to the bath Wayne had been demolishing. He stepped into the room, circling the empty wheelbarrow. Tile was piled in a corner, ready to be disposed.

The pedestal sink and toilet remained. An old medicine cabinet lay propped against a wall. I lifted the cover from the fixture, flipped it over, and showed him the underside. "Duct-taped here, inside a baggie."

He crouched, getting a closer view. "Hum," he grunted.

That's all you got?

"Where's the baggie and duct tape?"

"OMG! I threw it away. In the wheelbarrow." I gawked at the empty container. "It's gone." I groaned.

"Garbage day?"

I nodded, numb. "Did I throw away evidence?" I asked, a sick feeling in my stomach.

"Maybe. We don't know what this means. You didn't toss the tape and baggie to hide something, did you?" His eyes locked with mine.

"Hide what?" I was indignant.

"Katelyn, did you dispose of the packaging intending to hide a crime?" he asked, in a measured tone.

"Good grief. No! It was grimy, that's all. What crime," I gasped.

"Don't know. Could be nothing, might be something. Have to investigate," he said, satisfied. "You can put the cover back."

"What do you think?" I asked, my stomach queasy, my nerves on edge. I had gotten nothing more than a grunt about the photo, and a grilling about the discarded packaging.

"I'll be in touch," he said.

"Hello?" We heard Myra's voice from the entry.

"In here," I called. I picked up the porcelain cover.

"Sheriff?" Myra asked, "So nice to see you."

"It's my pleasure." He smiled.

"Katelyn gave you the photograph?" she asked, pausing at the entry.

I'm right here.

He held it up.

"What do you think?" she asked, her head tilted, expression thoughtful.

"Don't know if it means anything," he said with a small smile, his eyes hooded. He studied the photo.

"That's what I said." She nodded firmly.

Okay, I'm going to barf.

"Doesn't hurt to investigate," he said.

"I completely agree, Sheriff." She nodded again, her chin firm.

At my audible sigh, she grinned at me mischievously. “I’ll check out the upstairs while you two chat.”

“Say hello to your brother for me.”

“Oh, I will,” she assured him and headed for the second floor.

“Take care, Myra.”

“You too, Sheriff.”

“I’ll be off, Katelyn.” Don cleared his throat, and was all business as he placed the photo in the envelope.

“I’ll see you out.”

At the door, he said, “I’ll call you.” With a smile stretched across his face, he ambled to the porch and down the steps to the sidewalk, treating me to a view of his broad shoulders.

I was watching so intently that I didn’t hear Myra come up behind me.

“Nice,” she said, following my gaze.

I jumped about a foot and gasped. “Don’t sneak up on me!”

She smiled a Mona Lisa smile. “What are we doing today?”

“You’re keeping me company. I’ll be cleaning the basement.” I retrieved a copy of the picture from my bag, “Before I forget, this is for your brother.”

“Thanks. I’ll get it to him.” She took the photo, folded it, and placed it in the pocket of her jacket. Her movements were slow and deliberate, I could see the gears turning inside her head.

“What?” I was bewildered.

“Let’s have a cup of coffee before we begin,” she said, cautiously.

“You mean before I start,” I joked.

She studied me. Her expression pensive.

“Myra, I was kidding.”

"I know you were. Let's take a minute. We need to talk."

Oh my God. What now?

CHAPTER 12

Myra and I strolled to the porch. She sat in the chair, and I rested on the cold cement half-wall. She held her coffee mug with both hands, and I copied her position, waiting for her to talk. When she did, her speech was deliberate and halting.

"Katelyn, there's something I have to tell you about this house."

"Okay." I gazed at her, bewildered. "You mean something besides it's been the rehab from hell, and it's haunted, according to nearly everyone?" I tried to make light of the situation. She was making me nervous. When I get nervous, I try to joke and fail miserably.

"I wouldn't call the house haunted. I'd call it cursed."

"All right." My eyebrows rose. Those were strong words coming from Myra. "Why?"

"It was my mother's home." She sipped her coffee, her gaze clouded.

"Your mother? I thought you were part of the Johnson Construction Company? You grew up at the Johnson Family compound on Lake Minnetonka?"

"That was later."

"Okay." I waited for her to continue.

"My mother was widowed. She was in her twenties when my father passed. She had me to raise, and we lived with my grandmother, also widowed, in this home. We lived here until my mother met, and married, Roland Johnson, the construction mogul, who raised me."

"How does that curse the house?" At the same time, *wow, nice break, marrying into a rich family.* It was as if she read my mind.

"Coming from meager means, it was a challenge fitting into a wealthy family. It was not easy. My adoptive father's family thought she was a gold digger and never let her forget where she came from. She was fortunate to have hooked my father. That was my stepfather's mother speaking."

"Gosh, Myra, I'm sorry. I never knew it was like that."

"Yes. Well, we survived." She coughed, clearing her throat, and I waited, still puzzled about how that could curse the place.

"I loved my grandmother and have many happy memories of living in the home before moving to the estate on the lake. I visited my grandmother frequently as my stepfather's family barely tolerated me."

"I'm sorry," I said, and shook my head.

"Yes. Well...my grandmother took in renters and did other odd jobs, like ironing to pay expenses after my mother married the wealthy heir."

"Okay."

"In those days, women did not work outside the home. A woman without a husband was judged harshly."

"Yeah. I get that," I said, sympathetically.

"My mother tried to slip her what money she could. But my stepfather kept a close eye on the finances. That was a big reason she insisted I go to college. 'Never depend on a man for money,' she would say."

"I agree. Excellent advice."

"One of the men she rented to had a young child. The man paid for room and board and for my grandmother to care for his daughter."

"Uh huh." I sipped my coffee and studied Myra as she spoke.

"One day, I went to my grandmother's house, excited to visit the girl. I didn't have a little brother, yet," she said, remembering. "Grandmother told me the child and the man had moved out. After that, she became very ill. After she died, my mother sold the house to Ruston Ahoe's grandparents. The same Ruston, who admitted to killing his young tenant, but was never convicted."

"Okay. That doesn't mean the house is cursed," I said, puzzled.

"Later, after my mother passed, I found two obituary clippings in her things. One was for the man who had rented from my grandmother. The other was for the child."

"Oh, my," I gasped. "What happened to the girl?"

"She had a very high fever. The doctors with their treatments and medicine could not break the temperature. She died in her sleep." Thoughtful, she sipped her coffee, fingering the curve of the handle.

"Awful!" I gulped, and asked, "How did the man die?"

"He died in a freak accident in the garage."

"A freak accident?"

"He was working under the car, when the jack slipped and the car fell on him, crushing his head."

"That's terrible!"

"Yes. It was. Unbelievable, because just a week earlier, the child had died."

"Yikes! In the house *and* the garage?"

"Yes." She nodded and winced.

"You knew all this before I bought the place?" I asked. "And, you knew about the double jeopardy case?"

"Yes." Myra sounded reluctant. "Katelyn, I knew you could breathe new life into a house that had been damaged. I loved this home. I didn't know until much later what happened with the renter and his daughter. Grandmother wanted to protect me."

"Your mother kept the clippings? Why did she do that?"

Myra paused, then spoke deliberately, "I believe the gentleman was my mother's lover, and the girl, my sister."

"Oh. My. God." I let out a deep breath.

"So, you see, that is why the land, house, and garage, is cursed," she wiped a tear from her eyes, smoothed her hair, and rubbed her hands on her jeans.

"So, what do I do?" I asked, alarmed by her disclosure.

"You're in charge of removing bad karma," Myra said. "I'll leave it to you to find the best method." She rose and strolled inside. I hopped down from the half wall and followed her.

My head was swimming. Myra's mother had a secret lover, and daughter who had died on the property. Myra hadn't always been wealthy. It was overwhelming. My brain was brimming with the new information.

"I'll get started cleaning the basement," I said. I headed for the cellar, stopped, and threw my arms around Myra. I felt her stiffen. Although she had unburdened herself to me, she was not a hugger.

Physical labor is a kind of magic that frees the mind to work out problems. I brushed bleach on any dark spots on the wood. The bleach would kill mold spores. While I scrubbed the rest of the basement with borax and water, I pondered remedies to clear the house of its hex.

Satisfied with my progress at the end of the day, I sniffed the air. The vinegar containers had done their job. Any hint of mustiness was gone, and I had a plan to banish bad karma.

While I worked in the cellar, Myra loaded the tile from the bathroom floor into the wheelbarrow with gloved hands, careful to avoid construction debris. I smiled at her efforts to keep the dust at bay as she put the last piece of tile into the cart.

"Wayne will empty it tomorrow," I said, nodding towards the container.

"Perfect." She removed her gloves and brushed her jeans and jacket. "How about dinner at Popov's?"

"I thought you'd never ask." Suddenly, I was starving. The prospect of a big juicy burger danced through my mind, "I'll meet you there."

"Later." Myra was out the door.

I hurried to the cellar for one last glimpse of the progress. I moved a jar of vinegar to a better location and heard a click. The lights sputtered. The cellar went black. I gasped, all senses on alert. I was thrown into near darkness with fading daylight from the narrow windows. My eyes adjusted to the dim light and I headed to the stairs and fumbled for the wall switch. I flipped it off and on. Nothing.

"Dang it!"

Gripping the side rail, I felt my way to the top of the stairs, grasped the doorknob, and twisted. The door handle came off in my hand. I gasped and cursed again. Hyperventilating, shaking, I carefully placed the knob back in the doorframe, hoping to reconnect the mechanism, and open the door.

"Awaaaaaillll," a low sound started, and rose to a yowl.

I jumped and heard the other part of the knob hitting the floor.

"Who's there," I yelled, my voice trembling.

"Awaaaaaaaillllll!"

"Who is it?"

The knob rattled, and the door flew open. "It's me, Katelyn!" Myra stood at the doorway to the cellar. "What's going on?"

"Ahh," I gasped, startled. My nerves calmed. I was never so happy to see another human in all my life. "The lights went out, and the doorknob broke off. I heard noises!" I babbled and fell into her, wrapping my arms around her shoulders. She stood stoic, then took my arms, one at a time, and put them down at my side. She reached over and flipped the light switch. The lights blinked, then stayed lit.

"Get the electrician back. Let's go!" She grabbed her handbag, her back stiff, and stomped outside to her vehicle.

I snatched up my purse and followed on her heels, locking the front entry. Still trembling from being locked in the dark basement and the sounds of an eerie cry, I started the engine.

Ready to pull into the street, I stopped when I spotted the vagrant Myra and I had seen days earlier. He cut through the backyard wearing the same khaki army fatigue jacket and beanie hat. Our eyes locked for a millisecond. He pursed his lips, his goatee jutting. He glanced away. About to leap out of my car to confront the bum, he took off at a fast trot.

"I'll have to put up a fence," I muttered. "What is with this guy, anyway?" I left for the restaurant.

I waited until we were face to face at Popov's, with a glass of chardonnay in hand. "Thanks for getting me out of that jam."

"No problem. For once, I'm glad I forgot my purse." She sniffed.

"You and me, both." I cradled my glass and leaned in. "I heard something, Myra. I know I did."

"What do you think it was?" she asked, her expression sober.

"It sounded like a trapped cat." I shuddered, recalling the long, shrill, yowl. "It was creepy. You didn't hear it?"

"No." Her tone was firm. "The electrician needs to check the switch again. Has the knob been wobbly?"

"I hadn't noticed. It could have been. It is an old house. We've been preoccupied getting the basement cleaned up. Most of the time, the door has been ajar with the traffic."

"We'll inspect the cellar with Wayne tomorrow, see if we can spot anything amiss. I am sure he can fix the doorknob. Maybe there *is* a cat living down there." She laughed nervously.

"Okay." I nodded, relieved at the thought Wayne could fix the handle and check out any sounds.

Our burgers arrived, and we munched hungrily. We were nearly done before I asked a question which had bothered me while I cleaned the cellar.

"Myra, why do you think your grandma's tenant was your mother's paramour, and the little girl, your half-sister?"

She put her glass down, and sat back, with a wistful expression. "I was very young. My memories are fragmented. I recall mother being plump and full in the stomach when we were living with my grandmother. There was a dark-haired, handsome fellow, laughing. She was happy." She picked up a fry.

"Why didn't she marry that guy, and not your stepfather?"

Myra swallowed, and spoke. "My mother was beautiful. It was her draw and her burden. She was fickle, and that was tolerated because of her beauty. My grandmother represented my mother's lover as a renter. She helped her hide the pregnancy. She wore baggy clothes and stayed out of sight.

"Mother, lovelier than before the baby was born, started to work for my stepfather's company as a receptionist. My stepfather was attracted to her, and she kept the new baby a secret." She smiled and sipped her wine. "He was prepared for one child, not two. He told his family my mother had a daughter from a husband who had died in the war, in service to his country. Not that she had two daughters, one out of wedlock, which was scandalous at that time.

"My stepfather wouldn't have married her, so she did what she could to provide for the baby, and keep her lover at bay. She was swept off her feet by the construction company heir. She thought she could provide a better life for the girl if she married into a monied family. Maybe, she thought she would bring the child into the fold later. I don't know." She shook her head. "My grandmother helped her keep the baby a secret."

"Nice grandma."

"She was a saint," Myra agreed. "Shortly, after the child and man died, grandmother became deathly ill. I think the guilt she held for her part in the sham led to a premature death. After she passed, my mother sold the home."

"To Ruston Ahoe's grandparents?"

"Yes. Ruston inherited it after they died. He had lived in the dwelling for a couple of years before they found Skye Jones dead."

"It was when Ahoe was on trial, and the jury's decision dominated the news that he lost the house?" I asked.

"Yes," she said.

I pushed my plate aside. “Makes sense, he had to pay legal fees.”

“I want to bring the home back to happier times. To when my mother was happy, and we felt like a family,” Myra said. She finished her burger, and drank the last of her wine.

“She wouldn’t *ever* have married the other fellow, her lover?”

“No,” she said. “She needed a secure future that a man from a wealthy family could provide.”

We sat in silence, and I digested the story. It amazed me Myra had a scandal in her background. She had always been so prim and proper. Now I understood that we were both products of dysfunctional families. She got me.

“I’ve been thinking about what we might do to remove the curse,” I said, brightly.

“And?” She bit her lip, waiting.

“I think a séance is in order.” I clasped my hands together on the table. “It would be stronger than a cleansing, but less costly than ghost busting,” I submitted. “We can do it ourselves. According to Mr. Google, we need three people, a table, candles, and someone to summon whoever might inhabit the house or roamed the grounds to tell them to leave.”

“Whatever.” She groaned. “I’m still skeptical.”

“You said you thought the place was cursed.” I frowned, and reminded her, “You wanted to dispel the negative energy.”

“Yes. I suppose I did,” she said, nodding. “A séance, it is. Who will be our third person?”

“I could ask Wayne? He’s convinced there’s a ghost.”

“You don’t think it would freak him out?”

“I’ll see what he says. Otherwise, we may need to hire a medium.”

"Oh my." Myra appeared as if she needed another glass of wine. Her complexion paled, and she fell quiet.

"The cleansing worked with the Bluebird house and Ariel's renovation. A séance has got to be better," I urged, enthusiastically.

"Oh boy." She nodded, her decision made, "Let me know when and where."

CHAPTER 13

I caught up with Dan, the electrician, the next morning before I left for the renovation. He said he would be over later that day. When I arrived at the rehab, Wayne was hard at work in the master bathroom. He had emptied the wheelbarrow and was sweeping construction dust. He appeared rested after having the previous afternoon off.

"Something happen with the basement door, Kiddo?" he asked, puzzled.

"Yes. I'll tell you after setting up the fans."

My conversation with Myra about a cat living in the basement was fresh in my mind. I marched to the cellar, armed with a flashlight. I ran the light behind the washer/dryer, water heater, and boiler. The ceiling was open-beamed. Holding my breath, I ventured into the storage room and aimed the light along the shelves and failing cement wall.

After looking high and low for an opening or place a cat might take refuge, I put the flashlight down. My imagination was in overdrive, stressed by the renovation problems, and being trapped the day before. I had to get a grip.

I switched out the fans with ones Wayne, and Myra supplied. I collected the rental fans and dehumidifier and loaded them into the car. Then, I waved Wayne to the porch for a break. We stood outside, and I explained, "The lights went out when I was working in the cellar. The doorknob fell out in my hand when I was about to leave."

"You gotta be kidding!"

"No. I would not kid. I was lucky that Myra forgot her purse and came back. She rescued me." I laughed, nervously.

"Oh man! I'm sorry I left you here!"

"It wasn't your fault. I've called the electrician to check the switch again. If you could fix the knob, that would be great. Did you notice it was loose?"

"Can't say I did. The door's been open most of the time while drying out the basement," he said, his expression anxious.

"Sure." I tried to sound reassuring, but I was still a little unnerved. I had used the flashlight to focus into the crooks and crannies. The overhead light worked while I changed the fans. I didn't mention the noises.

"Heck, I can check the box."

"That's okay. I want to know if he left the window open when he was working." I was afraid I sounded loopy and didn't want to alarm Wayne any more than necessary, so I quickly changed the subject.

"You look better," I commented.

"Yep, feel heaps better," he said, relaxing. I waited as he dug in his shirt pocket for cigarettes. He lit up, took a drag, exhaled, and said, "Talked to Gillie about the mailman."

"You did?" I asked, surprised.

"Yep. Had to get it off my chest."

"Good." I nodded. "What'd she say?"

"Said it was nothing."

I felt a twinge at the back of my mind.

"'Taint nothing and I believe her!" he declared.

"If it clears the air, then that's all that matters. You have to trust Gillie."

Verify, then trust.

"Congratulations on having the courage to ask."

"Thanks." He grunted.

"Wayne, I have a favor to ask," adding, "You've said this place is haunted?"

"Yep." His voice was low, face pale. "Never had such problems at a job before. It's cursed!" *Myra had used the same term: cursed.*

"Myra and I have decided to have a séance, and we want you to be part of it," I blurted.

"Whaaaat?" He raised his head, cigarette in one hand, and studied me over the rim of his glasses.

I met his stare.

He took a long drag from his smoke, nodded, and said, his face pale, "If you think it would help. I'd do just about anything to get this house cleared of bad vibes. I'm not afraid of no ghost."

"Thanks, Wayne. I appreciate it."

"No problem. Let me know." He squashed his cigarette on the bottom of his shoe, stood, and said, "I'll take a gander at that doorknob. Then take out the toilet and sink." Everything, except for the antique, claw-footed tub, would be replaced. He started for the house.

"Great. I'll return the equipment. I'm a day late." I collected my handbag and hiked to the car. I drove to the rental store, unloaded the equipment, and paid the bill, gnashing my teeth at the extra charges. It couldn't be helped. I would add them to the growing list of unexpected costs to rehab the house.

Back at the rehab, I checked the cellar door. Satisfied the doorknob was secure, I ventured down to check the moisture levels with my new gizmo. The studs were drying out well. In another day or so, I was confident the wood would dry thoroughly.

While I was checking the moisture in the wood, Dan from Dynamic Electric, arrived.

"This switch the culprit?" he yelled down.

"Yes."

He clattered down the stairs and threw the circuit breaker for the basement electrical, then went back to the switch.

I watched him remove the wall plate.

"Here's the little bugger," he said, and fixed the connection.

"Dan?"

"Yeah?"

"Did you open a window on the second floor when you were checking the wiring?"

He replaced the plate on the switch and frowned. "Don't quite remember. I do a lot of jobs." He flipped the breaker. The lights and fan started up.

"But you could have?"

"Not likely. Is there a problem?" He stared at me.

"No." I backed off under his frown.

"Okay." He brightened. "Fixed the switch. No charge. Missed it somehow."

I guess that's a break, anyway. Even he couldn't remember opening a window.

"Thank you."

Dan left. The cellar had not lost its creep factor. I shuddered at the roar of the fans and headed upstairs.

Wayne removed the pieces of the fixtures to the dumpster.

When he came back, I said, "Let's call it a day."

"Sounds good." He nodded, grabbed his jean jacket, and slipped it on.

I hurried to the basement to turn off the fans. When I emerged, "I thought tonight would be a good time for the séance. Would that work for you?"

"The sooner, the better." Wayne stood straight, his eyes grave behind his glasses, his chin out. He gave a nod and snorted.

"I'll check with Myra and call you."

"Ya betcha." He nodded again and headed out to his van. I locked up and watched him drive away.

The séance was on my mind as I navigated the city traffic. I wanted to finally rid the home of bad karma, ghosts, or curses. The internet was my source for removing lousy juju.

At home, I poured over the web's directions for seances, which were pretty user friendly. I decided against using a Ouija board. Being superstitious, the warnings about how it could serve as a portal for unfriendly entities put me off. I did not need foreign beings entering the dwelling through the Ouija board or by any other means. I mulled over how to perform the ritual for an optimal outcome.

Satisfied I had a plan, I dialed Myra, "How does this evening work for a séance? About nine o'clock? At the house?"

"Seems like a respectable time. But why not midnight?" she countered, dryly.

"That's a good point. Maybe that would be a better hour. On a night with a full moon," I quipped. I was determined to keep a sense of humor through this adventure.

"Let's not go overboard. We have no idea what we're doing."

"Do you doubt this, Myra?"

"No. No, not at all." She was a little flip.

"Because the instructions say if there are any doubters, the ritual won't work."

"No. It's fine." Her tone left me uneasy as I hung up. But, because of the sage burnings we'd done at the other houses, I dismissed the feeling. They both worked admirably, despite her reluctance.

I called Wayne. "The séance is set for nine o'clock tonight at the rehab. I'll drive."

"I'll come over."

In a flurry of activity, I fed Boots, cleaned up, and printed directions for the ritual I hoped would get my Hiptown renovation on track.

Rap, rap, rap.

"Hey, wifey. Are you in there?" Eddy called. My stomach lurched. It was never good when Eddy called me 'Wifey.'

"What's up?" I opened the door.

He stood in the corridor, expression contrite, his eyes lowered. He shuffled his feet, "Can I come in?"

I motioned him in.

"I wanted to let you know as soon as possible..."

My eyes narrowed, and I closed the door, observing his long, lean body, and disheveled, dark brown hair. I sniffed the air. "You've been drinking."

"No. I had a beer."

My eyebrows raised, I viewed him suspiciously. "Why are you here?"

"Got fired today."

"Oh no!" I groaned. I recalled the last time he had shown up unexpectedly. He had surprised me by paying the full rent on the Bluebird home after saying he couldn't. "This happened today?"

"I got a warning last month." He avoided my glare.

"You knew this was coming?" My tone accusing.

“No, not really. They gave me probation. I kind of blew probation,” he muttered, his head down.

“What d'you do?”

“I didn’t show for a mandatory meeting.”

“Why not?” I demanded.

“It was my only day off. I worked three weeks straight, and the hitman they hired pulled a meeting on my one day off. I didn’t think they meant it.”

Mute, I studied him. After a lengthy silence, I conceded, “That was a crappy job. I’ll make coffee.” I had had my share of crummy jobs with evil bosses. What else could I say?

I went to the kitchen and started a fresh pot, thinking about Eddy’s dilemma, which would be mine, because if he couldn’t make the rent, I would be stuck doing survival jobs again to make the payment. I would fall behind on the Hiptown renovation. Mentally, I calculated my bank balance as I prepared the java.

I took a mug of fresh coffee to him as he sprawled out on the sofa. His deep brown eyes muted with gloom.

“Hitman, huh?” I hid a smirk as I sat in the chair across from him.

“That’s what they called him.”

“That’s who they get to cull the herd, cut the fat.” I snickered. Leaning against my chair, the absurdity of it hit me, and I stifled a laugh.

His eyes lit up, and he caught my snickers and gave into a rolling belly laugh.

“We’ll figure it out, Eddy.” I wiped tears of mirth from my cheeks. “Right now, I have a séance to get to.” I checked my watch and gulped my coffee.

“A what?” He sat up, at attention.

“A séance. At the Hiptown house to banish the bad juju that’s causing all the renovation problems. It’s been a giant headache.”

"Cool. Can I come?" His dark eyes sparkled and his face full of hope, and something else. Mischief.

"I don't know if that is such a great idea."

Rat-a-tat! It was Wayne's knock.

I opened the door, "Kiddo, ready to go?" He looked past me to Eddy. "Yo! You in on this, too?"

"Sure thing." He leaped from the sofa.

"I'm not so sure..."

Eddy was up and out the entry, chatting enthusiastically with Wayne, while I lagged, gathering the candles and directions. At the last moment, I grabbed Skye's diary from the coffee table and locked up. *Oh, boy, this is going to be good.* Resigned, I followed the two men to my car.

We crammed into my compact ride, Eddy in front, and Wayne squeezed in the back seat. I parked on the street in front of the dwelling. Myra waited in her spiffy SUV while the three of us piled out. The street lamp cast an eerie glow on the facade of the renovation. The air was chilly and damp. A light wind blew, ruffling tree limbs.

Myra opened her vehicle and got out slowly. We met on the sidewalk. "Hi, Eddy. Welcome to the séance." Myra's tone dry.

"Thanks, this is great," he whispered, his voice quivered with excitement. The four of us trooped to the front entrance.

"Here," Wayne said in a hushed voice and held up his cigarette lighter to illuminate the lock for the key.

"Thanks," I said. "Why are we whispering?"

"Cuz, it's creepy," Eddy said, this time in a normal voice.

That broke the tension, and we entered the house, flipping on the lights.

We surveyed the space. The place was a wreck. The foyer leading to the living area bordered a bare-bones kitchen. The worn kitchen appliances had to be disposed of. The wall separating the kitchen and the living area had been removed and needed patching. Flooring needed replacing or sanding, if possible. It was bereft of a table or chairs. The master bathroom was stripped to bare walls with just the tub remaining. The wheelbarrow waited for more debris.

It was dismal.

"Maybe, the best place would be the upstairs bedroom where we found Skye's diary," I said. "We can sit on the floor."

"I have a blanket in the car," Myra said. "I'll get it."

"Perfect," I said. Wayne, Eddy, and I trooped up to Skye's old bedroom. While we waited for Myra, I placed the candles and instructions on the window seat, along with Skye Jones' journal.

"So, how's this work?" Wayne asked.

"Yeah?" Eddy chimed. "What do we do?"

Myra's footsteps sounded on the steps. She entered the room with a red-plaid car blanket and I helped her spread it.

"Myra and I have learned our rituals have to be flexible," I said.

"Preferably, with wine," she added.

"Sorry, no wine," I said. I went to the bench and grabbed the votives and directions.

Myra sighed.

"First, let's all sit in a circle," I said.

In unison, Myra, Wayne, and Eddy sat and crossed their legs. Myra faced me.

On my knees, I placed the diary in the center of the circle, laid out the candles and sat down between Eddy and Wayne.

"According to the instructions, someone has to be the medium, and talk to the spirits."

"That would be you," Myra said. "You own the house."

"I am okay with that," I said. "Although, you have a long history with the home."

"Huh?" Wayne asked. "What do you mean?"

"Myra's mother owned the house before Ruston Ahoe's grandparents bought it. Ruston inherited it," I said.

"Well, I'll be..." He viewed Myra, who said, "Katelyn, you're the owner now. You have the most to gain from releasing whatever spirits might be here."

"Does everyone agree?" I asked.

"Yep," Eddy agreed. "It's your party."

"Or funeral," Wayne said, chuckling. He had a gallows sense of humor.

"How do we proceed?" Myra asked.

"Most seances have a formula; they open with a stated intention for the entity, followed by an invitation to the spirit. You close the session with gratitude and peace to the guests," I explained.

"Sounds simple enough," Myra asserted. "Let's light the votives and turn off the lights."

"You got it," Wayne said and handed me his cigarette lighter.

I lit the candles. Eddy rose and flipped the overhead light switch and sat in the circle.

"Let's all join hands," I said. Each of us held a hand out to each other. In our boy/girl/boy/girl group, Eddy squeezed my hand. His was warm while mine felt cold.

"Now, let's close our eyes and take a moment, and think about what we want to accomplish," I said. I closed my eyes, and everyone followed suit. I felt Eddy fidget and opened my eyes a slit. He was staring at the doorway behind me and appeared distracted.

"Eddy?"

"Sorry," he muttered and turned to the group, closing his eyes.

We sat, quiet.

"Well, Ms. Medium?" Myra asked, breaking the silence.

"It's coming," I protested. "Okay," I said with a deep breath, "we are here to ask the spirit of whoever occupies the house to make their presence known."

We remained quiet, waiting, and listening.

Nothing.

"I'll ask again." I cleared my throat, "If there are any spirits residing here, come forward and show yourself." I threw in a chant, "Ahem, ahem..."

"What's that supposed to be?" Myra asked in a quiet tone.

"It's a chant to summon the spirits," I whispered, hoarsely.

"Ha!" Wayne chuckled.

"Kind of a wimpy chant, Kate," Eddy said, and snickered.

"Okay. You chant," I said, glaring at him by candlelight.

"Humm, hum," he retorted.

"Kids, settle down," Myra chided. "This is getting out of hand."

Squeeeaaak! There was a dash of movement through the circle in front of us.

"AAAHHH!" Myra screamed and jumped to her feet.

"What was that?" I yelled. Gasping, I rose and flipped the light switch. Wayne unfolded his legs, and Eddy leaped up.

"It was a mouse!" Myra shrieked.

"Guess I'll need to get some traps," Wayne said, surveying the room.

Eddy chuckled.

"Myra, are you okay?" I asked.

"I've had enough of furry creatures," she complained as she dusted her slacks. "Between raccoons and now mice in this place," she sputtered.

"I'm sorry, Myra," I said.

"It isn't you," she said, resigned.

"I think our spell has been broken. The only spirits out tonight are the mice. I don't believe they are the sole source of the problems with this house. Let's go," I said.

"Amen," Myra agreed, her mouth set firmly. She stood stiffly, hugging her midsection.

"Yep, fine by me," Wayne said. He snickered and jabbed at his glasses.

"Got no argument here," Eddy said.

I squatted, blew out the candles, and collected them. Hesitating, I placed Skye's journal inside the window bench, making a quick sign of the cross. Wayne and Eddy observed my actions, ill at ease.

"It's a suitable place for the diary, for now," I said. Truthfully, the volume made me uneasy at home.

"Sorry," Wayne offered. "Thought this might be the ticket to getting rid of the ghost."

"Yeah, Kate," Eddy agreed.

"I am not," Myra said, with a sniff. "This isn't the proper atmosphere."

"It isn't. Part of the directions say you can't have doubters, or the ritual won't work," I said, pointedly.

"We'll chat," Myra said in a brittle tone, gathered her blanket, and led the way to the main floor.

Great, now Myra is mad at me. I followed her, with Eddy and Wayne behind me.

BAAAM! The sounds of slamming startled us halfway down the staircase. We stopped in our tracks. A gust of wind blew up the stairwell.

"Oh my God!" I said, inhaling. "What is it?"

"Door," Wayne said.

"Sounded like it came from the kitchen," Eddy chimed.

"I'll check," Wayne said, "wait here." He brushed past Eddy, Myra, and me.

"I'll come with you," Eddy said and followed Wayne.

Myra and I stayed on the staircase, waiting for the men to return.

"A spirit might have shown up, after all," I murmured to Myra. Her face drained of color as she considered my remark.

"Whatever," she grumbled.

Wayne returned; Eddy trailed him.

"Kitchen door was unlocked," Wayne said. "Ain't no good reason for that," he groused. "Nobody came in that way."

"I did, when I got the blanket," Myra said, "I'm sure I locked it."

"Let's get out of here," I urged. "Wayne, it's secured now?"

"Yep," Wayne's head bobbed, his mouth pursed, and he stroked his bristled chin.

Eddy's eyes were bright, and he said, "Shut tight as a drum."

"Let's go!" I said. Myra sprinted the remainder of the stairs and out, saying, "I'll call you tomorrow, Katelyn."

"Thanks, Myra." She let the door slam.

"Kate?" Eddy asked.

"What?" I stopped.

"Don't you have to do something?" His eyes were full of mirth, and he playfully batted his lashes.

"What?" I demanded.

"Thank the spirit for coming?"

"Thank you! Amen!" Once again, I crossed myself. "Now, let's book!"

Okay, Eddy, when did you become the expert on seances?

CHAPTER 14

Wayne, Eddy, and I piled into my vehicle. From the safety and darkness of the car, we studied the home.

"That was awesome, Kate! The place really is haunted!" Eddy said.

"Come on," I said, resigned. "We had a skeptic in the séance."

"Myra," Wayne said.

"She's probably right. The door was unlatched at some point. The house is old and creaky, and has mice," I reasoned.

"There's something stranger than a mouse," Wayne said, "but, I'll get the traps upstairs tomorrow."

"Thanks, Wayne."

"Wayne's right. The place is freaking haunted!"

"Uh huh," I muttered, trying to ignore the churning in my gut. I fired up the engine and drove home.

When we arrived, Wayne said, "We had quite a time, tonight. Tomorrow." He gave a brief salute and left Eddy and me outside my entry.

"Mind if I bunk on the sofa tonight, Kate?"

I waved him inside. "Take the spare room."

"Thanks, Kate. You're the best." He sauntered to the second bedroom. He had painted the room and gotten it into shape as part of his keep before renting the Bluebird house. Boots meowed and followed him. I could tell he still smarted from the "hitman" incident at his job, and it would be nice having company after the failed séance.

It was a little after ten thirty. The event had taken less than two hours. My nerves were shredded. I needed some quiet time and a large glass of chardonnay. I poured a glass and settled into the sofa, reviewing the evening's events, while Eddy's muffled snores echoed from the guest room. I sipped the wine and mulled over the séance, searching for anything I might have missed.

Rap. Rap. Rap. I jumped, checked the time, and leaped to the door. Frowning, I peered through the security opening.

It was Don. He was out of uniform and wore a casual jacket over a soft blue shirt. I opened the door.

"Good evening, Kate. I hope it isn't too late." His blue eyes warmed me, and butterflies fluttered in my stomach. He was an oasis of sanity, tall, blond, and calm. John Pardi's tune, "Heartache On The Dance Floor" sounded in the back of my mind.

As the lyrics ran through my head, Eddy popped out, "Hey, Wifey. I need a glass of milk." He ruffled his bed tousled locks on the way to the kitchen, dressed for sleep in his white skivvies.

"Oh, hey, Sheriff," he said, passing the two of us.

My head dropped, and I closed my eyes, exasperated.

"Hey, Eddy," Don said.

"How's the hot car?" Eddy asked.

"Great."

Eddy rattled around in the kitchen cupboard, taking an eternity to find a glass and pour milk.

"'Night," he said and strolled back to the guest room, tumbler in hand, and closed the door.

"How about a ride?" Don smiled; his eyelids lowered.

"Perfect. I'll get my coat."

Don shifted smoothly while I rode in the passenger's side of the Corvette. Our bodies moved with the motion of the gears. He entered the freeway, heading north, and picked up speed. I watched the speedometer creep to eighty miles per hour.

"We're speeding. The limit is seventy mph," I called. It was noisy in the tight front seat with the wind and speed.

"It's the interstate, everyone does seventy-five in the right-hand lane," he said.

"Okay, but you're the sheriff, driving a hot car. A red Corvette," I protested.

"That, I am," he grinned and slowed down.

"Hungry?"

"I could eat."

"Let's eat," he beamed, and I felt my stomach flutter again.

At a tiny town about a half hour north of the cities, we pulled off the freeway into the parking lot of a twenty-four-hour diner.

We settled into a booth, and he ordered two eggs over easy, sausage, wheat toast, orange juice, and coffee. I requested pancakes and coffee.

"I suppose you want to know why we're here?" he asked, fixing his gaze on me.

"It's not because you wanted breakfast?"

"Nope," he chuckled and sipped his coffee. Reaching into his jacket pocket, "I found some information about your girl." He pulled out the photo I'd given him of the teenager with the wide eyes and blue drop earrings.

"She was reported as a runaway by her family in Snake Hollow," he said. "Her name is Willow Rivers. She was seventeen when she went missing, and was never found."

"So, she's still a missing person?"

"Technically, yes."

"Technically?"

"It's a cold case. After this long, with no contact with her family, or law enforcement, it doesn't look good."

"She could be gone...?"

"Dead."

"Oh dear. Why would her photograph be in the house?"

"Don't know," he said, gravely. The color of his eyes dimmed.

"Maybe Ruston Ahoe had something to do with her disappearance?" I asked. "He killed Skye Jones and got away with it."

"Yep. Doesn't mean he killed anyone else. Doesn't mean this girl is still missing. Maybe she's made a new life for herself."

"But the picture was stashed under the tank cover in Ruston's bathroom. And he got off scot-free with killing Skye!" I sounded like a broken record. It bugged me. The 9-l-l operator said it was Daemon in the background, saying he would kill Skye if she talked. At the time, there wasn't any evidence that pointed to Ruston.

"You don't know who hid the photograph, or why," he cautioned. Our food came.

"True," I conceded, digging into pancakes.

"You don't know if the hidden picture has any connection to her as a missing person."

"Where is Ruston Ahoe, anyway? Can't police bring him in for questioning?" I countered, peevishly.

"Ask him what? Ask him about a photo of a missing girl found in a house he hasn't lived in—for how many years?"

"A few," I said glumly. "No one's lived there since he lost the place four years ago. It was vacant until I bought it. Logically, it seems he would know something. He was the last occupant." I was determined.

"Investigators need more than a picture to interrogate someone," Don countered.

"So, the police need something that ties Ruston to the photo. Like fingerprints?"

"Yes. They dusted the photo and envelope." He put his coffee cup down and met my gaze.

"And?"

"The prints they found belonged to Skye Jones."

Speechless, I thought quickly to her diary. She hadn't written about another female living at the house.

"How can that be?"

"Skye got into trouble with the law when she was a kid. She ran away, stole some jewelry, got busted. That's why her fingerprints were on file."

"That's rough." I frowned. "But we don't know why her prints are on the envelope." He stared at me.

"No, we don't. Let's go." He stood and threw down money for the tab. I grabbed my purse and followed him.

He drove home in silence. The freeway was a blur while I pondered the sheriff's news that the prints on the photograph and the envelope belonged to the dead girl, Skye Jones.

CHAPTER 15

I was in the kitchen the next morning, getting ready to head to the Hiptown rehab when Eddy popped out of the spare room, dressed in jeans and a flannel shirt. He helped himself to coffee.

"What's the plan?" I asked, surveying his attire.

He flashed a disarming smile, "I'm going to get a job."

"Good!"

Wayne's *rat-a-tat* sounded. Relaxed, Eddy opened the door, mug in hand.

"Yo, Eddy." Wayne nodded. Then he turned to me. "Kiddo, think I should pick up the sheetrock this morning?"

"Sounds good. We're ready to hang drywall in the bath and the main living area," I said, with a nod. I grabbed my bag, threw the straps over one shoulder, and gripped my coffee mug.

"Sheetrock?" Eddy squealed. "I love sheetrock!"

"Since when?" I demanded; my eyes narrowed.

"Hey, you want to help me this morning?" Wayne turned to me, "Kiddo, I could use a little muscle. Unless you are set on moving drywall?"

"I suppose," I said, with an eye-roll. "It's not like I haven't hauled drywall before."

"Nope, sure ain't," he said. "But if Eddy wants to help?"

"Okay. I can work on the budget while you guys get the drywall. But Eddy must find employment so he can pay rent on the Bluebird property. He can't stay," I warned him. *There I go, the wife voice.*

"Sure thing, Katie." Eddy eagerly followed Wayne out.

"Sheetrock is cool." I heard the excitement in Eddy's tone as the men talked, their voices fading as they strolled the hallway. With a sigh, I put my handbag on the table. All this male bonding with Eddy, Don, and Wayne was disturbing.

Boots strolled from the guest room where Eddy had slept and rubbed his body against my legs.

"You too?" I got out kibble for the cat.

I settled in at the table, sorting through the pile of bills, listing others that I still expected. My renovation was a money pit, along with the eerie stuff that kept happening.

With Don's revelation that Skye's prints were on the envelope I'd found, and Eddy out of work, my anxiety level was rising. I put the stack of bills aside and left for the project. I needed Eddy to become gainfully employed, pronto.

As I parked in front, the locksmith's van passed my car. The driver honked. About to get out, I stopped. Fast Freddie was at the wheel. He quickly waved, and I returned the greeting.

Wayne's vehicle was in the driveway. He and Eddy were pulling sheets of drywall from the back and carrying them through the porch into the living room.

"Maybe, I could help you hang the sheetrock?" Eddy asked Wayne, with an edge of excitement.

"Might be good to have a helper. Have to ask Kate. She's boss."

Eddy watched me, his brown eyes sparkling with anticipation.

"Would it move the job along faster if Eddy helped today?" I asked Wayne. "Just, *one* day."

"Sure would."

I hesitated. I had agreed to let Eddy load the drywall, thinking he would go on his way to find employment, but I sighed, and relented. "Okay. I'll take a few bucks off the Bluebird rent for working today." If the drywall went up faster, that would make up for his help.

"That's great, Kate!" His face broke into a wide smile. "You won't regret this."

Oh, boy.

"Did either of you see where the locksmith was working this morning?" I asked.

"Nope," Wayne answered.

"Me, neither," Eddy said.

"Huh," I said. "There may still be a vandal around here."

"Yep. Wasn't no good reason for that kitchen door to be open last night," Wayne said.

"Myra may have left it unlatched," I offered.

"I s'pose." He nodded. "But Myra doesn't seem like she'd forget to lock up," Wayne added, stubbornly.

"No, she doesn't," I agreed. "I'll check it. I hate to pay for re-keying locks again."

I hustled to the kitchen and studied the back door. I wasn't sure what I was looking for. I tried the lock. It opened and closed like a standard deadbolt. *Myra had to have left it unlocked. She was in a rush.* It was the only logical explanation.

I could go to Big Mart and get a new lock. That would be easy enough to install. It would mean one more key to keep track of. But it would be cheaper than Fast Freddie. I shelved that idea. If it happened again, then I would replace it.

I strolled to the front entrance. Fast Freddie's van was parked two houses up. Curious about why he was in the area, I hurried to catch up to him. When he limped to the driver's door, apparently finished with his appointment, I waved him down.

"Hi, Freddie, how's business?" I called.

"Hey!" His dimples in full view, his gaze magnified by his eyeglass lenses.

He paused, resting one leg on the door's jam, ready to get into his van.

"Did something happen?" I asked, gesturing at the residence he had just come from.

"Hey, yeah. Lady's purse was stolen, had spare keys in her handbag, ID, credit cards, the whole deal. She was pretty upset."

"Oh, dang. That's awful."

"Hey, yeah."

"How'd that happen?" I frowned.

"She doesn't know. She figures it was taken in broad daylight. Said she hadn't locked her door, and her purse was just gone. Vanished."

"Double dang!"

"Yeah."

"She thinks it was a burglar?"

"Near as she can figure. She tore the house apart, car, everything." He flashed another broad smile. "Hey, how're the new locks?"

"All right. If everyone would remember to use them," I said. "Someone forgot to latch the kitchen door last night, and it flew open. It was windy, and it scared everyone half to death. With the place under renovation, it's spooky."

"Hey, yeah. I know what you mean." He smiled shyly. "Does the upstairs bedroom still have a window seat?"

"How did you know?" I inhaled, stopped, startled, and observed him.

"I rented a bedroom from the guy who used to own the house, Ruston Ahoe. That man who killed that girl."

"You did?" My voice rose. My shoulders tensed.

"Sure did."

"When?"

He glanced away, his head lowered, and said in a quiet voice, "I lived here the same time as Skye Jones. They charged me with her murder."

"You? I thought the guy's name was David, Daemon...something like that?"

"It's Daemon Pleasant. Pleased to make your acquaintance," and he stuck out his hand. I shook it. His grip was cold and clammy.

"You said your name was Freddie when you changed my locks," I said, accusingly, my nerves on edge. My stomach sank, remembering the company was an LLC, and I had not found an owner's name. Mentally I kicked myself for not searching for the owner, especially since he could move in and out of houses freely. I tried to reassure myself. *He was licensed, bonded, and insured.*

"Hey, it's not a lie. To my customers, I am Fast Freddie," he said. "It's a business. Bought the company from Freddie, just kept the name. Makes it easier."

"Why tell me, now?"

"You seem like a nice lady. That place is haunted. I wouldn't want anyone to get hurt."

Why would he say that? I felt a chill.

"You think Skye is haunting the house?" I asked. My nerves tensed.

My guard was up, and I wanted to run, but Daemon's admission and implication that the house might be dangerous, made me dig in and grill him.

"Hey, I'm not a religious man, but if someone beat the rap for murdering me, I'd be haunting the place. For sure." He said it with such simplicity it rang true. *Exactly what I would do given the same circumstances.*

"Okay," I said. "But this is an investment property. I am a Home Rehab Specialist. I need to fix this house up and sell it. This is my career. I doubt most people would consider a ghost a selling point."

"Hey, I hear you. But you got to make it right with Skye," he said. "I did time because the cops told me if I didn't fess up, I'd get thirty years in the slammer. My lawyer said eight years was a good deal. What could I do? I was there. She was dead. 9-1-1 had a recording of me yelling at her. They had nothing on Ruston. They didn't know Rusty, and I went waaaay back, to high school."

"You were friends, not just landlord and tenant?" That had not been in the news account of the murder.

"We didn't hang together. Rusty ran with the smart kids." He smiled, his dimples deep, and said, "I was a stoner."

"You smoked marijuana?"

"And other stuff." He grinned at me.

"Oh."

He shrugged and smirked.

"But Ruston confessed to killing Skye after they acquitted him."

"Yes. He did. I have to thank him for fessing up. He was my get out of jail card. But, hey, what if he hadn't gotten off? What if he hadn't confessed?"

"So, you and he didn't have a deal?" I asked, tentative.

"A deal?"

"Yes. You take the fall. I'll get off, then confess. We both go free."

He threw back his head, laughing so hard, his cap with the 'Fast Freddie,' logo fell off. When he finished chuckling, he picked up his hat, soberly. "I couldn't count on Rusty getting off. I took the best deal I could get. He rolled the dice, and it paid off for him and me. Ruston Ahoe is as close to Satan as you or I will ever see."

"Why did he confess?"

"We were tight once." He shrugged.

"How was that?"

"But, hey. That's done, now." He flashed a dimpled wide grin.

Daemon's cellphone jangled. "Gotta go. It's a customer." He nodded and limped to the driver's side.

I said goodbye to Daemon, and trekked back, my mind whirling. I did not like the fact he hadn't been honest about his name. Although it was common to keep an established business name, he had let me believe it was his. A lie of omission.

His lawyer had counseled him to take the deal. If a jury convicted him, he would spend a bigger chunk of his life behind bars. He was scared, and may have been manipulated by a deceptive friend and landlord.

I had to put the encounter with Daemon, aka Fast Freddie, out of my mind. I had a project to finish, and a house to sell. Two houses, if Eddy didn't get a job soon. Not to mention banishing a ghost from the premises, according to just about everyone except Myra.

On the porch, the sounds of the radio came from inside. True to form, Eddy had the radio blasting. The station was playing classic country, and he sang along to an old Ronnie Milsap tune, "What A Difference You've Made In My Life!"

"Hello!" I shouted over the radio.

The men were in the master bathroom. Eddy held a sheet of drywall in position, while Wayne secured it with a drywall screw.

Preoccupied by their task, they didn't see me. I hiked to the cellar to check on the level of dampness. Trying the moisture meter again on the floor and wall studs, I was relieved to see everything felt, and measured dry.

I viewed the basement and considered how to make it more family friendly. Better lighting was a priority, but cleaning the windows, painting the floor, and fixing the flaking cement would have to do for starters. The dark, dank cellar gave me pause. I shuddered and headed upstairs.

"Myra called!" Wayne yelled when he spotted me and turned the volume down. I breathed easier with the quiet. "She wants you to call her."

"Okay. How's it going?" I examined the new drywall in the bathroom.

"We're moving right along. With Eddy here, we should get most of this done today."

"That's great, Wayne. Did Myra say what she wanted?"

"Naw, just to call."

I dug for my phone in my pocket, wondering why she hadn't dialed my number. The cell registered a missed call. I fiddled around with the phone and found, somehow, the setting had switched to silent mode. Such are the wonders of technology.

"Hi, Myra. You rang?"

"Yes. I'm sorry about how I acted last evening."

"You don't have to apologize. It was a lot to take in," I protested.

"That's true. But I want to make it up to you. How about lunch at Popov's?"

"That sounds great." The sounds of classic country blasted from the bathroom where the men worked. *A restaurant would be reasonably quiet.*

"Is Eddy there?" She asked.

"How d'you know?"

"The loud music," she said, with a chuckle.

"Uh huh."

"Shall we meet up at one o'clock?"

"Sounds wonderful." I hung up, relieved she wasn't angry about the disastrous séance.

I collected the mouse traps from the basement. With Wayne and Eddy occupied with hanging the sheetrock, it was my job to set the snares for the rodent that disturbed our ritual. I grabbed the jar of peanut butter and marched to the second floor. I set up the traps, using the food for bait, placing them anywhere that could be a mouse path. Finished with that chore, I evaluated my progress in the rooms. The upstairs bedrooms were done, except for painting and final cleaning. The floors looked great. Newly refinished original hardwood floors always enhanced a room. Next, I would start taping the walls for painting.

I met Myra at Popov's. We were quickly seated. I opted for a light lunch, a bowl of wild rice soup, knowing I would be returning to the project to paint.

"So, Eddy's working at the renovation?" she asked, after we settled in with mugs of steaming java.

"Just for today. He's helping Wayne with the drywall."

"Really." She sounded skeptical.

"I know." I sighed. "He's unemployed, again."

"Oh, boy."

"Yep," I muttered.

"I'm sure he'll work it out. He's a survivor," she said, and sipped her coffee.

"Yes." I nodded.

"I am sorry I was the unbeliever at the séance," Myra said.

"It's all right. None of us have ever done a séance before. I'm sure there's a learning curve," I protested.

"I have another idea." Her expression serious, she paused.

The server dropped our food and hurried back with refills. I waited for Myra to continue. I spooned the soup and met her gaze. "What are you thinking?"

"A ghostbuster."

My spoon slipped from my fingers and splatted back into the soup. I sat back and stared.

"A what?" I gasped.

"It makes perfect sense. If there is a ghost, we need the services of a ghostbuster." Myra *looked* sane. Her hair was styled with new highlights. Her complexion glowed with a facial. She was, as usual, impeccably dressed. I wore my work attire of blue jeans and a sweatshirt, covered by a jacket.

"If I didn't know better, I would think you had lost your mind," I said, my tone still high.

"Now, now. I've done some research, and a competent ghostbuster runs about $500."

I groaned at the figure.

"I will pay for it," she said, her voice clipped and firm.

"Myra, that's a lot of money for something that isn't proven. There are logical explanations for what's happened."

"How do you explain the door bursting open?" She asked, arching one brow.

"You said yourself, you 'thought' you locked the exit last night. That raises a level of doubt."

"And Boots? Why was he freaked out? You said he was staring at something? Something you or Wayne couldn't see," she countered.

"Boots *was* miserable. He was out of his element," I protested. "He doesn't do change well."

"What about the basement windows? The flooded cellar?" She stared me down.

"Could have been a vandal. Fast Freddie, the locksmith who is actually Daemon Pleasant..." Myra looked bewildered as I prattled on, "said a thief stole a purse from a residence. It happened during daylight hours."

"The flickering lights? The hissing circuit breaker?" She continued to grill me.

"The electrician fixed the wiring. To the tune of..."

"How did the doorknob come off in your hand? You were trapped in the cellar! Do not argue, Katelyn Baxter. I will do this. If there is nothing to worry about, then this won't hurt."

She had me there. When Myra used my full name, I knew I had to back off.

"The money is a fair amount," she conceded, "but there have been so many sad events in the home, besides being a renovation nightmare. I believe the house has seen happenings more tragic than sage burning, or a séance can handle."

"Since when have you been so involved with psychic phenomenon?" I asked, on the defensive. I hated for her to spend money on something unproven.

Her face sagged, and she was mum.

"Is it because of what happened with your mother and her paramour?"

"It would be my way of making peace for my mother, the child, and her lover."

"Okay." I leaned back. Myra admitted that she doubted the ritual. She wanted the whole enchilada, a ghostbuster. She believed the place was cursed. Who would have thought? She was the logical one. I had the bohemian mother who lived in a commune and an ooky, spooky sense of the unseen.

"Set it up." I shrugged.

"Good," she said decisively. "What did you mean by the locksmith?"

"Fast Freddie is really Daemon Pleasant. He kept the company name."

She wrinkled her nose. "That name seems familiar."

"Daemon is the tenant who took the fall for Skye Jones' murder."

"He is? No!" She inhaled.

"He seems to be an amiable fellow. A little naïve, gullible. I think that's what got him hooked into taking the rap."

"And now he's a locksmith?"

"Everyone has to work. He thinks the place is haunted, too," I said. "Me, I just want to get this project moving. We've had too many delays, too many expenses," I complained.

"Getting the spirit out once and for all should do the job."

"Okay, Myra." What Myra wants; Myra gets.

CHAPTER 16

On my way back to the rehab, I stopped at the hardware store, and picked up two gallons of antique white paint. The label promised it included primer. With stir sticks, brushes, and masking tape, I added another bunch of money to my credit card.

It was after two o'clock when I parked on the street in front of the renovation. I trekked to the hatch, lifted out a can of paint, grabbed the bag of supplies, and marched to the back. I would avoid walking through the main floor with my supplies. Eddy and Wayne were likely hanging drywall in the living area. Country music blared from inside.

I strolled past the garage to the kitchen access, my purse straps slipping off my shoulder. Weighted down by my materials, I stopped and stared at a figure slipping from the back exit. It was the beanie-hatted man with the goatee and khaki colored jacket. He spied me, started, and froze, his eyes beady.

"What are you doing! Who are you!" I shrieked.

He smirked, his thin lips pursed, his hooked nose prominent, his eyes narrowed to slits. He started for my bag.

"Awwwwwk!" I gasped and dropped the bag with the supplies. I held my purse with one arm, lifted the paint can by the handle, and swung it at the assailant's face. The edge of the container hit the side of his jaw. He fell back and rubbed his chin. Scowling, he grunted and lunged at me.

I let my bag slide further down my shoulder, recovered the can, gripping it to my chest, like a basketball player trying to sink a layup shot. I aimed the canister at his chest, the most substantial part of the skinny man's body. The can flew out of my hands.

He ducked and threw out a long thin arm to block the can.

"Aaaaaaaaah!" I screamed, snatched the canister from where it rolled to the man's feet. Ignoring my bag lodged in the crook of my arm, I leaped and thrust the paint bucket with all the force of my five feet, five-inch frame, aiming for his head. He ducked. My handbag swung wide and hit his man bits. He doubled over, screaming, and fell to the ground. Again, I grabbed the container by the handle as it rolled away. I swung it towards his head again. I missed. The creep kicked at my legs.

"Aaaaaaaah!" I shrieked, and toppled, hitting the sidewalk, and hoped someone would hear my screams over the music.

There was a blur. Then Eddy jumped on the back of the intruder, forcing him back down. The scoundrel squirmed under his hold. Eddy grabbed one arm, then the other, and gripped them together, pinning the interloper to the sidewalk. The vandal continued to flail under his grasp.

Wayne propelled from the kitchen exit, "Whaaaa?"

"Stop him, Wayne!" I yelled. The interloper twisted and grunted under Eddy's grip. Wayne plunked his body on the man's legs, restraining him.

I dug for my cell phone in my purse, which I'd kept a death grip on while fighting the imposter, and dialed 9-1-1.

"What is your emergency?"

"We've got an intruder! Send help!" The goateed vandal flopped from side to side like a fish, while Eddy held his arms and Wayne gripped his ankles. My voice wavered as I shouted, afraid the man would escape.

"What is your location?"

I shouted the address and stayed on the phone until I heard police sirens.

A squad car screeched to a stop in front of the rehab, and two police officers jumped out. Eddy and Wayne lessened their grip, and one police officer slapped cuffs on the scofflaw. Wayne and Eddy straightened after the man was secured and brushed off their clothes.

The cops stood the vagrant upright, marched him to the waiting squad car, and placed him in the back seat. One officer returned with a pad, and asked, "What happened?"

"I caught that man leaving the house!" I gasped. "He was trespassing! He tried to steal my purse! You need to search him!"

Wayne and Eddy waited while I babbled to the officer about the fight.

"He must be the guy who vandalized the house! I bet he got in and opened the windows during the storms. The entire basement was a mess! I reported it!"

"We'll check our records. Good thing you made a report." The officer nodded. "We'll search him. You must come to the station and press charges for assault and trespassing."

The officers left with the interloper cuffed and stuffed, while the man's hooded gaze sparked fury, secured in the police car.

"The house was open?" I asked Eddy and Wayne.

"Yep," Eddy said. "We were working. Didn't think we had to lock up."

"It doesn't look like he got anything," I said. I shuddered, remembering the seedy-looking man lurching for me.

"He was probably trying to steal money. A purse or a wallet," Wayne said, grimly.

"Yes. He went for my purse. Let's walk through the rooms, see if he took anything."

We trekked upstairs, the main floor, and the basement, investigating until we were satisfied everything was as it should be.

"It appears nothing is missing," I said. "I bet he thought he could sneak in and snatch something while you two were working. If he was casing the place, it would be easy to see workers through the windows. With the music cranked up, you guys couldn't hear him. He could take a quick peek and leave. He didn't count on anyone else coming."

"Gutsy scumbag," Wayne said.

"Or desperate," I said. "You and Eddy have your wallets. He didn't get my bag." Even if he had, my credit cards were almost maxed out, and last time I checked, I had about twenty-five cents in cash. Myra had paid for lunch.

We took a break on the portico with a fresh cup of coffee. I sat in the chair, and the men rested on the half wall.

"I guess you're happy I was here, huh, Kate?" Eddy sputtered. He was psyched, his energy high, and I was exhausted. Wayne was pensive.

"Yes. It was good you were here."

"Maybe I could work on the house? Help you get it ready for market? I won't charge extra for bodyguard services," he teased, his eyes twinkling.

"Eddy, I can't afford you."

Silence. Wayne broke the quiet, and heaved a sigh of relief, "Well, Kiddo. Guess we found our ghost."

"Yes." I brightened. "It must have been the vagrant. Myra and I saw him using the backyard for a shortcut through the neighborhood. I saw him one other time. Maybe," and I shuddered, "he was even sleeping in the house."

Wayne snorted. "He sure might have."

Eddy groaned.

"Let's call it a day." I rose. "Let's lock up."

Wayne left in his van. I drove away, with Eddy in the passenger's seat. I felt terrible. I couldn't afford to hire him, and there was an uneasy silence as I drove home.

"Sorry, Eddy. I can't swing a helper," I said, parking in the garage stall.

"That's okay, Kate." He opened the door and swung long legs out. "I'll get a good job."

"Thanks for today," I called. He let the door slam and sauntered to his pickup. He hopped in and gave a brief salute, grinning as he drove off. Eddy would be fine.

Wayne lingered in the hall outside of Mrs. Gilman's unit. He smiled. "Gillie's cooking tonight." She poked her head out, "Hello, Katelyn," and sniffed. She wore a powder blue matching hoodie and sweatpants outfit, one of her many standard getups.

"Hello, Mrs. Gilman."

Wayne entered, and she shut the door behind him. I glanced at the closed door. *At least they seem to be working things out.*

"Yowl!" I opened the house to an anxious Boots. He studied me with his tail up, and he nuzzled my leg with a meow.

"You wouldn't believe the day I've had." I stroked the cat and filled his bowls.

After I showered and unwound with Boots on the sofa, I called Don.

"YOU DID WHAT?"

"Now, calm down. What was I supposed to do? Let him grab my purse, steal my money, and take my identity?" I had called him, thinking he could tell me who my intruder was. And that I would ask what would happen after I filed charges. I was mistaken. He was reading me the riot act.

"YES! That is EXACTLY what you should have done! NEVER stop a thief or an intruder. GIVE him your purse. SAVE yourself. He could have had a gun, or a knife, and made mincemeat out of you. He is a criminal, for God's sake! Desperate men do desperate things.

"I couldn't stop. My reflexes kicked in," I protested. "Besides, he wasn't armed."

"That was sheer luck!" he retorted.

"Could you find out who the scumbag is, please?"

"I guess. Why?" he grumbled.

"I have to get this house fixed up and sold. The intruder must be behind the awful goings-on and the negative juju in this home. If he is engineering the dreadful events, then its problem solved. It makes sense," I reasoned, "Besides, another woman in the neighborhood had her purse stolen from her home during the day."

"Where d'you get that?"

"Fast Freddie, er Daemon, the locksmith told me. He was changing the locks for the neighbor whose purse was taken."

"Who?" He sounded skeptical.

"His name is Daemon Pleasant; he owns Fast Freddie's Locksmith. He kept the business name when he bought the company."

"That name sounds familiar," he said.

"Fast Freddie?"

"No. The other name."

"He was the tenant who went to jail for the murder of Skye Jones."

"Seems like you know a lot about this guy."

"I have that kind of face. People tell me things," I said blithely. "He was innocent, so he didn't have any reason to hide it. He appears gullible and had a bad lawyer. He unloaded on me because he knew I was the new owner."

"Harrumph."

"He thinks I'm a nice lady."

"Harrumph."

"Will you check out the vandal, please? It's worth a pizza and a beer," I promised.

"Katelyn, are you bribing an officer of the law?"

"Not if it's a Hawaiian pizza," I hedged.

"Yeah. That's no bribe." He laughed. "I'll see what I can find out."

My next call was to Myra.

"We've got our ghost," I announced.

"What?" Her tone was breathless.

"I stopped an intruder sneaking from the back exit at Hiptown."

"You what?"

"Remember the man we saw running through the backyard? The skinny guy wearing a khaki jacket and beanie hat, a scuzzy goatee?"

"Yes?"

"He's been breaking into houses." I told her about the afternoon's events, ending with, "So, there's no need for a ghostbuster. I'm sure he's the one who's been causing all the mischief at the project."

"You think it was him?"

"Positive, Myra. It will save you money. I appreciate it, though."

"All right. I can use the funds to pay the technician for replacing my family room windows."

"What?"

"This afternoon, a gaggle of geese made themselves at home in the family room. They broke the window and left a huge mess!"

"No!"

Myra's home was gorgeous. Her view of the lake was hypnotic.

"Yes." Her voice tight. "I was about to call a cleaning service."

"I'll let you go."

"We'll chat soon. Should I call my brother to see what he can dig up on the prowler?"

"Guess it couldn't hurt. I asked Don, though."

"The sheriff will handle it. He's such a nice man, Katelyn."

"Yes, Myra." I disconnected.

I didn't know where Don and I stood as far as boyfriend/girlfriend. But his concern about the interloper made me feel all warm and fuzzy inside. I slipped into bed, satisfied I had solved the mystery of the ghostly presence at the rehab. And pleased Sheriff Don Williams cared enough to get angry about my stopping a criminal in the act.

CHAPTER 17

"What in the world...!" I gasped. Wayne and I had just entered the renovation. I followed the sounds of running water, stepping on wet floors. Water seeped from the closed kitchen sink cabinet.

"Yee gads!" He ran ahead of me and threw open the cupboard. A supply line squirted liquid over the inside of the cabinet like a fountain. "I'll get the main!" He dashed to the basement to shut off the water.

"When will this stop?" I shouted out of frustration.

"Sorry, Kiddo. I usually close the main at night. We left in a hurry." Wayne was back and apologetic.

"Yeah. I know," I groaned. "Think you can fix it?"

"Yep."

"Okay." I breathed a sigh of relief. He could replace the part. The wood cabinets were empty and would dry. Now for the rest of the stuff. I examined the area where the wall had been removed for the open concept living area. Wayne had put the finishing piece of drywall in place and taped the new seam. The section had been ready to mud and sand. Now it was waterlogged.

I checked the master bathroom. The bottom of the new sheetrock hung in the bath was soaked too.

"Might be able to trim off the lower sections, save some of it," Wayne speculated.

"Okay." I sighed, tired of the constant setbacks. "I'll move the paint cans and supplies out of the way." I mopped up water and dried the bottoms of the paint containers with a cleaning rag.

"Basement's soaked, too," Wayne said. "Water seeped through the kitchen floor."

"Drat!" I said. I left a can on a riser to the second level and trailed him to the cellar.

"How bad is it?" I asked, coming up behind him.

"It's wet, all right," he said, somberly. From my vantage behind him, I saw water had pooled in the middle of the cement floor.

"Dang it!"

"How 'bout I get started down here. You work in the kitchen?"

"Yep. That will work," I sighed again, weary of the never-ending assaults on the renovation.

"I'll get the wet vac from Matilda," Wayne's name for his work vehicle.

"Do you have any more towels?" I asked hopefully.

"You're in luck. Just picked up a bunch of cleaning rags from the home store."

"Great."

"I guess it could have been worse," I said finally, viewing the mess. "We won't have to rent the extractor again."

"Yep. It ain't good, but not as bad as the flooded basement."

"It's an old house, stuff happens. Right?" I asked, my resolve still firm to get this rehab fixed up and sold.

"Sure 'nuff does."

I followed Wayne outside to his van. He handed me a bag of towels from the back, and I trudged to the house. He unloaded the shop vac and carried it to the cellar.

Rap. Rap.

I had been cleaning for about an hour, my jeans and shirt damp, my hair sticky. I headed to the front door. Someone nudged it from the other side. Don peered from around the edge.

"Should lock this," he chided. He forced the door open and walked in.

"Yeah, yeah," I answered, brushing my hair from my face. I felt my face do a slow burn. I placed my hands on my hips, ready for a fight.

"What's going on?" He frowned, observing the pile of drenched towels I had thrown in the wheelbarrow. Later, I would wring them out in the bathtub, then home to wash.

Wayne had finished with the shop vacuum to remove the pool. Once again, the fans were roaring, drying out the cellar. It was lucky I'd kept the spare fans at the house. The main floor was nearly dry with my work on towel duty. Now, he was on his knees, crouched with his head under the sink, taking apart the supply line.

"Broken water line," I muttered.

"Bummer," he said. Don was in uniform and appeared unruffled. His cobalt eyes scanned my hair and face. "Ruston Ahoe is the fellow who assaulted you and tried to steal your purse. Thought you'd want to know."

"You're kidding? The same man who got away with murdering Skye Jones?" I gasped. "He's changed!" The clean-cut, beak-nosed, brown-haired, all-American guy wearing a pullover sweater, found in my Google search, didn't look at all like the scruffy man I'd caught running from the kitchen exit.

"He has," Don conceded. "He lives with his mother, not far from here."

"Great. What happens now?" I shrugged, dismayed at the sheriff's news.

"You press charges. He goes before a judge. The judge decides if he can get bail."

"I suppose his mom bails him out?" My voice rose with disgust.

Don smiled at my distress, and his sharp gaze softened. "Bail depends on the judge. A judge has to follow the law."

Interrupted by knocking at the entry, we stopped talking. Myra waved from the entrance, then sniffed, and surveyed the mess in the open concept living area.

"I thought you'd be painting," she said, puzzled. "What happened?" She smiled at Don and said, "Hello, sheriff."

"Myra, how's your brother?" He tipped his hat and grinned.

"He's good."

"Say hello for me. I was just leaving." He pivoted. "We'll be in touch, Katelyn."

"Okay. Thanks for stopping," I snapped, irritated by the news of Ruston Ahoe.

Myra shot me a mischievous smile as the sheriff left. Through the open exit, she watched him stroll to his police car parked on the street.

"What?" I feigned.

"What happened?" Myra ignored my protest, examining the room.

"Water line broke."

She stepped gingerly over the damp floor and saw Wayne, his head tucked into the cabinet.

"Wayne's fixing it," I said.

"Almost got it apart," his voice muffled from the cabinet. "Hi, Myra." He poked his head out. "This is it!" He dangled the plumbing part in one hand.

"Excellent!" I exclaimed.

Myra nodded in agreement. "What did the sheriff want?" She asked.

"He said that the man who broke in, nearly stole my purse, and assaulted me is Ruston Ahoe."

"Oh, my!" she exclaimed, her eyes huge. "Then Ahoe couldn't have broken in and done this. He is in jail. We still need a ghostbuster."

"It was a busted line," I protested. "It is an old house."

She stood firm, staring me down. Wayne shrugged into his jean jacket and was ready to leave for the plumbing supply store, "Might not be a bad idea."

"Hey, wifey!" Eddy waited at the entry.

I closed my eyes, nerves on edge, trying to compose myself, "What is it, Eddy?"

"Whoa. Chill. Just came by to see how the rehab was coming. My company called. They fired the 'Hitman.' They want me back," he said, with a huge smile.

"You're kidding. That's wonderful!"

"Hey, Eddy, that's great," Wayne said and guffawed. "Sometimes, things work out."

"Yep. 'Hitman' threatened to sue the company, human resources got involved. They wanted to know what he did to me. Bunch of the other guys complained. So, the hot shots did it to save their butts."

"That's wonderful," I said. "That means you can pay the rent on the Bluebird place."

"Sure can," he said, his eyes twinkling. He spotted the soggy drywall. "What happened?"

"Busted line," Wayne said. "Say, Myra's gonna get us a ghostbuster. You in?"

"On a ghostbuster? You bet!" Eddy was giddy.

"There's no ghost," I said, my voice brittle. My resolve weakened as Myra, Wayne, and Eddy stared at me. "It's just bad luck. A whole lot of rotten luck. Pure and simple." Their stares never wavered.

"Oh, all right!" I threw up my hands. "Set it up."

CHAPTER 18

"It's time we took control of this situation," Myra said. We were tucked away in a booth at Popov's to go over the plans for the ghostbuster. She sipped her wine and set the glass down. Her brow furrowed.

"Myra, everything that's happened in the house has a reasonable explanation. I hate for you to do this."

"Not everything; there's still Boots' reaction." She tapped the side of her glass.

"He's a cat."

"I think you have to consider the sheer number of events, besides a plausible explanation," she said, firmly. "The home had the reputation of being haunted, even before you bought it. Let's deal with it, and put a stop to the energy, whatever it is."

"Okay." I sipped from my wineglass and leaned back against the wooden booth.

"I have a name of a ghostbuster. His name is Randy. His company is Ghostbusters R Us. These days, they call them paranormal investigators. Minnesota has several locations where unusual activity has been observed."

"Really?" Myra was getting into this. And I thought I had the gypsy leanings.

"Uh huh. The treatment center is probably the best known."

"The old mental institution."

"Exactly. Many years ago, when patients died, they were buried on the grounds, with a number. No names."

"Ghastly," I said. "But can't they rid the grounds of their spirits? That's what we want."

"That's a severe case. I doubt there are that many entities haunting the Hiptown house."

"Let's hope not." I suspected this had more to do with Myra's mother's paramour and half-sister, and Myra's guilt about surviving and thriving.

"I'll call him. His website says he has special equipment that focuses on any strange happenings."

"All right." I didn't know what happened if you disturbed a ghost, or *if* there was a ghost. The prospect made my stomach seize. I pondered the idea, and fingered my empty stemware while we kibitzed.

"This organization has excellent reviews. I'll set it up for this Saturday night." Her hair, as usual, was fresh, her sweater draped across her shoulders, a perfect fit at the shoulder point, an infinity scarf around her neck. I had come from the rehab in work duds.

Sitting back, my thoughts in a whirl, I watched Myra's expression. She had always been the level-headed model of maturity against my less than stable upbringing. I had looked to her for advice and as a sounding board. I was afraid she might be going off the rails with the house.

"Are you okay?" Myra asked, watching my face.

"Are you sure you want to do this?" I asked, my stomach queasy.

"Positive." She was firm, tapping her glass with a manicured nail.

"Do you think you might be a teensy bit too invested in the possibility the place is haunted?" I asked, breaking under her direct gaze. I gulped. Confrontation was never my strong suit.

"Because of my mother's boyfriend, and the child?"

"Yes," I said and took a big gulp of wine.

"I might be," she admitted. "There was always a shadow over my childhood, growing up with a wealthy patriarch. There were too many unanswered questions, too much darkness over what should have been a joyful time. My mother had the security that money provided, but she was never happy."

"Okay," I said, finally. "I'll be happy if this ghostbuster can put an end to the renovation disasters and give a measure of peace to Skye Jones *if* her spirit is trapped there."

"So, we're on the same page?" She added, "You need the house cleared of spirits to sell it, and I want a peaceful exit of any bad karma from my mother's ill-fated relationship."

"Yep." I added, "Myra, your mother must have been a babe."

"Hussy," she said, her brows raised.

"What?" I asked, surprised. I blinked.

"My mother was a hussy," she said crisply. "Now," she warned, "I will never speak of it again." Her rosy cheeks turned a bright red.

"Myra, let's get a ghostbuster."

Saturday evening came, and I waited in the porch area of the renovation with Myra, Wayne, and Eddy. I clung to Skye's journal while we waited. Earlier, I had retrieved the stashed diary from the bench for the evening's activities. The night air was warm. Summer had begun. There were fragrant petunias, geraniums, and a soft breeze. A full moon and twinkling stars lit up the inky sky. I connected the outline of the little dipper and inhaled the scent of late blooming lilacs from a bush that adorned one corner of the home.

"This is pretty cool," Eddy commented. Wayne was guarded. He took a deep drag from a cigarette and kept silent. My stomach was churning. I knew the color from my face had drained in response to the turmoil in my gut. Myra was the only one who appeared to be sure and steady in this quest.

"They should be here," she said. "There they are." A dark blue van stopped in front of the rehab and parked. The driver hopped out and strode the sidewalk to the house. Under the light of street lamps, he looked to be in his thirties. He was on the shorter side, with a mass of brown hair. He wore a navy T-shirt with white block lettering declaring Ghostbusters R Us. His companion stayed in the van.

"Myra Payten?" he asked at the bottom step leading to the portico.

"I'm Myra." She extended her hand.

"Randy, Paranormal Investigator." He gripped her hand and gave it a hearty shake.

"It's nice to meet you. This is Katelyn Baxter; she owns the house. Wayne is the handyman doing the renovations, and Eddy. Eddy is Katelyn's...friend." She glanced at me. I shrugged and did an eye-roll. Eddy was Eddy.

"Glad to meet you!" Randy said. He stepped up and grasped each of our hands in a vigorous handshake. "My assistant and I will move the equipment. Where should we set up?" The sky dimmed, and clouds began to hide the stars. Light drops of rain began spitting with a flash of lightning. A distant boom of thunder rumbled.

"Where is the best place for the equipment?" she asked.

Wayne nervously guffawed.

"Is there somewhere that has had more activity than other areas?"

"The cellar," I said. "That's the space Boots freaked out in."

"Boots?"

"My cat."

"What did he or she do?" Randy asked, attentive.

"Boots is a male. He would not leave his carrier. He cowered at the back, hissed, and stared at something. I couldn't see anything," I said.

"Animals can be more susceptible. Their eyesight and hearing are much more sensitive than humans."

Great, maybe Boots did see something.

"Otherwise, a bedroom on the second floor," I added. "A girl who once lived there was killed by the former owner of the house."

"Ahh, there has been a tragic event." Randy spotted the brightly colored volume I gripped. "What is that?"

"It's the diary that belonged to the murdered girl. I thought it might be important." I held it out to him.

"Could be. Hold on to it while we set up."

I glanced at Myra, wondering if she wanted to add anything. She was silent, her face impassive.

"I'll get the equipment," Randy said. He hiked to the back of his van. The woman in the passenger's side hopped out, joined Randy, and helped him unload the apparatus. They walked to the entry, each carrying a case.

"This is Misty, my partner," Randy said. The young woman wore a matching navy T-shirt and jeans. She had short white hair, streaked orange, and a tattoo sleeve covering one arm.

"Hi, Misty," the four of us said in unison. She smiled and nodded in acknowledgement.

"What kind of gear do you have?" Eddy asked.

"We carry several types of gadgets," Randy said, as he accompanied Myra and me inside. He held the door for Misty, and Eddy and Wayne entered behind her. "A thermal imaging camera, wireless audio recorder, and an electromagnetic field detector."

"Awesome!" Eddy chortled.

Myra flipped the foyer light switch. In single file, I led the group to the basement. As we marched down the narrow stairwell, there was another din of thunder.

"Storm's picking up," Randy commented.

"Uh huh," Wayne said.

Randy and Misty surveyed the space. Everyone fell silent. I shuddered, overwhelmed by what we were about to do. Suddenly, the lights extinguished. Myra gasped, I puffed, and movement stopped.

"Oops," Eddy said, from the top of the stairs.

"Cut it out!" I yelled. Eddy's footfalls clattered on the staircase.

"It was a mistake," he protested, joining the group.

I relaxed and sighed. Randy studied the area.

"My cat fixated on the canned goods area." I pointed at the door.

"All right," He nodded. "It'll take a few minutes to set up. While everyone gets comfortable, I will place the recorder on the washer and the electromagnetic field camera at the front of the room. The thermal imaging camera can go here." He put the equipment facing the storage space. "That should cover all areas in the basement."

"I have one chair on the porch I'll get for Misty. Sorry, we'll have to stand or sit on the steps," I said. "We should have brought refreshments."

"You think?" Myra asked, her expression tight.

"Maybe, later," Randy said. "We must concentrate on anything that seems out of the norm. The equipment is pretty self-explanatory. The audio recorder will catch sounds the entity makes," he explained. "The imaging camera will record images of a being. And the electromagnetic field camera will register movement of electromagnetic particles."

Wayne made a muffled sound that could have been a chuckle, cleared his throat, and said, "Sorry. Tickle in my throat."

"Cool," Eddy said, and shifted from one foot to the other, his arms crossed.

I handed Skye's diary to Eddy, then dashed up the stairs and outside to retrieve the lone chair from the porch. I toweled off rain droplets and carried the chair to the cellar. I offered it to Misty, and she sat. Randy stood next to her. I snatched the diary back, and Myra and I sat on the cellar stairs. Eddy leaned against the wall and Wayne stood, his arms crossed.

Another crack of thunder echoed.

"Turn off the lights," Randy said. "Now, we will ask the spirits to show themselves, and wait. No whispering or noise, please."

I flipped the switch.

"If there are any spirits nearby, you may touch my hair," Misty announced, her voice solemn.

Shivering in the darkness, breathless, I clutched Skye's journal, stroking it as if it were alive, waiting for a sign.

A half an hour of waiting produced zero, zip, nada. No photos and no movements. The only sounds were of the six of us breathing. The quiet atmosphere was punctuated by a cough, a stretch, or change in someone's posture.

Eddy broke the silence first with a long yawn, and asked, "You think the spirit is asleep tonight?"

"It isn't unusual to have no activity. Paranormal entities can have lengthy periods of dormancy. Doesn't mean there isn't anything here," Randy said.

"Well, there's a limit to my budget," Myra said. "We will have to pull the plug on this for now."

Bammmm! In the distance, we heard a noise like a door slamming.

"Who's there?" I yelled, my heart pounding.

"It's upstairs," Myra said.

"The bedroom!" I jumped up, flipped on the lights, and led the way to the main floor. I scanned the area and bolted up the stairs to Skye's old room.

I threw open the door and hit the light switch. Eddy and Wayne were on my heels. Misty and Randy followed them. Both windows stood open a full six inches.

"I know I didn't open any windows!" I said, my voice quivering. "Did you?" I asked Wayne.

"Sure didn't, Kiddo."

I glared at Eddy. "Are you messing with us again?"

"Nope. Not me. I swear." He threw up his hands.

"Maybe, the windows are the gateway to the house for the spirit?" Randy suggested, viewing me soberly.

"That doesn't help," Myra said, frowning. She entered the room, lagging behind on the first floor. "We don't know if the ghost is in or out. We want it out."

"Why would a ghost open a window?" I demanded. "Wouldn't they float through the wall or a closed window?"

"It may be their way of announcing its presence," Misty said.

Wind whistled through the partially open windows along with a splatter of raindrops. Tucking the diary under my arm, I dashed to shut one window, then ran to close the other.

KABOOOOOOM! A tremendous boom resonated, shaking the home's foundation. The lights flickered and shut off.

"What was that?" I asked, trembling. The room was pitch black. In the murky darkness, Wayne took out his cigarette lighter and flicked it on, lighting the compact space. Myra found her cell phone and added more dim lighting.

"Sounded like a lightning strike," Wayne said. "Close by."

"It did," Eddy agreed.

"I'll check it out," Wayne said. Eddy trailed him. The rest of us trooped downstairs and to the backyard. The street lamps were unlit. We could see the yard between flashes of lightning and light rain. The wind whipped the tree limbs and shrubbery branches into a frenzy. Branches, leaves, and strips of bark littered the area.

"Lightning hit the big old oak tree. But the tree's still standing," Wayne said.

"Let's get out of here," I said. "Now." I collected my purse and stuffed the diary inside.

"I'm with you," Wayne said.

"Me, too," Eddy chimed.

Randy and Misty loaded their equipment. Myra met them at their van and paid them. By that time, the rain had stopped and Myra trekked to the porch where Wayne, Eddy, and I gathered.

"I'll say good night. Our work is done. Amen," Myra said. She gave a quick wave and hurried to her SUV.

"'Night, Myra," I called.

Wayne and Eddy chimed in, "Good night!"

"Can you help clean up this mess tomorrow morning, Wayne?" I asked. "Say, eight?"

"No problem, Kiddo. I'll be here." He left, driving Matilda, and I drove Eddy home.

"Pretty cool, huh, Katie?" Eddy stretched his long legs in the Festiva as I drove to the Bluebird house. "It was like a sign from God or something," he chortled. "The whole place and ground shook. It was awesome!"

"Eddy," I groaned. My nerves were on edge. "Give it a rest."

I pulled up, parked, and waited for him to get out. He leaned over and planted a kiss on my mouth and squeezed my shoulder.

"What's that for?"

"Old times sake." He grinned and left.

"Good grief," I muttered with a smile. He was irrepressible. If he wasn't so damn good-looking, and if we hadn't already been married....

At home, I gave Boots a treat, downed a large glass of chardonnay, and collapsed into bed.

CHAPTER 19

I met Wayne at the Hiptown house early Sunday morning. I bought a big thermos of French vanilla coffee and breakfast sandwiches from a fast-food joint. The day was bright and sunny. We tacitly avoided talking about the ghostbuster and the evening's events and worked at a feverish pace, raking and gathering the debris. By ten o'clock, we had most of the litter picked up and bundled at the curb for the waste removal truck. I breathed easier once the power came back on.

"Do you think I should remove the tree?" I crossed my fingers. A tree that size could run into a thousand dollars, or more, to fell and have the wood removed.

"It's a sturdy tree. I think it'll recover," he said.

"That's good," I said, relieved. "Thanks." I put the rake on the porch.

"No problem. I'll take off, then. Gillie and I got a date."

"Sure, Wayne. You kids have fun," I joked.

"Yep. We're doing pretty good." He grinned and headed for his van.

My cell phone rang.

"How about brunch?" Don asked. A little thrill jolted me. I countered with, "Brunch or breakfast must be the only meals you eat."

"Hardly," he returned. "I have a lead on the girl's photo you gave me. I thought you might be interested."

"Give me an hour." I hung up. I locked the rehab and drove home in record time.

Rushing to the bathroom, I showered, changed, and wrestled with my hair. Giving up, I put it up in a ponytail.

When he knocked, I was ready in my best jeans, Henley-style top, sandals, and handbag.

"Let's go," I said.

Don smiled. "What's the rush?" He waited while I secured the exit.

"You want to eat. I want to hear what you found." If truth be told, he made me nervous. I was still rattled from the night before with the ghost busting and lightning strike. Not to mention, I had had a few cups of java.

"Fair enough." His face creased in a grin, and the corners of his eyes crinkled.

He led the way to his hot car, with the top down, and opened the passenger door.

Moving smoothly through the gears, he maneuvered the side streets, heading to the interstate.

"Is Joseph's okay?" he asked, and glanced at my mane, grinning. My ponytail flew back with the motion of the vehicle and the wind ruffled his silver-blond locks.

"Great. Let's go."

"You got it." He drove, racing the freeway to Hidden Falls, about a half hour's drive. My right hand clutched the shoulder harness, the left arm across my midsection, gripping the door handle. He expertly negotiated the manual gears, coordinating with the clutch. I admired his driving. I had never mastered the art of a manual shift, grinding gears the few times I'd tried.

The Corvette's tires squealed as he drove into the restaurant parking lot. He stopped and cut the engine. He grinned at me. I relaxed my grip on the harness.

"You okay?"

"Fine," I croaked, catching my breath. Smoothing my locks, I got out, my legs shaky.

He smirked, met me at the passenger's side, and grabbed my elbow, guiding me to the restaurant.

The server seated us in a booth facing the parking lot, within view of the crazy fast Corvette. After we ordered and settled in with coffee, he studied me, as if he were thinking. "We found the girl we identified as Willow."

"Really?" I sat back and put my cup down. "Where is she?"

"Can't tell you. She doesn't want to be found."

"Why? How did you find her?" My breath catching. In the next breath, "Where is Skye's family?"

"Her family left the city after the verdict. That's all we know right now."

"All right."

"We tracked Willow from court records showing Willow Rivers changed her name when she married John Schmidt."

"Okay." I nodded. "Did you talk to her?" I inhaled.

He paused and took a long drink of water.

"Yes. I talked to her," he spoke in a low voice. "She says she has a wonderful life. She has children. She hasn't seen her family since she was a teenager. The short story is, she has no desire to dredge up an unhappy childhood."

"Did you ask her about Skye?"

"I did. She said she read about the murder in the paper."

"Did you tell her about the photo?"

"Yes. She said she does not know why her photo would be there, or why Skye Jones would have put it there. She didn't know Skye."

"But she was reported as a run-away about the same time Skye lived in the house."

"Her family reported her missing seven months before they found Skye." He gulped his brew.

"Could she be lying about being there, or knowing the girl?"

"I don't know, Katelyn. Don't know why she would lie. There's nothing to connect her with Skye's murder, or to Ruston Ahoe."

"I have to speak with her."

"Why?"

"Maybe, if she sees the journal, it would jog a memory."

"Let us presume she's telling the truth. She did not know Skye, and she wants to be left alone." He met my gaze firmly. His expression set and unyielding.

My face burned, thinking about the problems with the renovation, the floods, the open windows, getting trapped in the basement, the continual rehab problems. I had thought of Don more and more as a confidant. He would think I was an absolute looney, but I had to try. "There have been a lot of difficulties with the renovation. She may know something that could rid the house of its spirits." I spit out 'spirits.' The word gave me the Willies.

"Spirits?" His brows raised, studying me, long fingers wrapped around his mug. "Yes. The place has that reputation. But Willow is an adult and has a right to her privacy. I can't breach that right."

The server placed a plate heaped with eggs, sausage, hash browns, and toast on the table in front of him.

"This looks great!" He beamed, and dug into his breakfast with gusto.

I forked a bite of a Western omelet, savoring the eggs, ham, green pepper, and onion combination. After we stuffed ourselves and the plates were cleared, he asked, "How's Eddy?" He shot me a quick smile.

"Eddy's Eddy. He lost his job. He got it back. He leads a charmed life." I laughed.

"Yeah. I thought he might." He chuckled. He shifted in his seat, "You two have history?"

"We were high school sweethearts. We married when we were teenagers, divorced, and stayed in touch. I married Jake. He died." I threw up my hands, "Eddy's an orphan, kind of like me."

"Your parents are gone?"

"My father's dead. My mother lives in a commune. How about you?"

"Commune, huh?" His eyebrows raised.

I shrugged.

"Parents dead. No siblings. Never married. Came close once."

I sipped my coffee. "I'm sorry. You're an orphan, too."

"Guess so."

"What happened with the woman you might have wedded?" I blushed. I was being nosy, a bad habit.

"It was many years ago." His eyes took on a distant air, his mouth firm. He fingered the ring of his cup. "We were teenage sweethearts, like you and Eddy," he said, gazing into his coffee. "We'd just gotten her car from the garage. She had work done on her old Chevy. I was following her. Long story, short. It started snowing, the heavy, sleeting stuff." He paused, then spoke quietly, "An eighteen-wheeler skidded across the center line, slammed her vehicle into a highway barricade. She never saw it coming. Died instantly."

"That's terrible," I gasped. "You saw the entire incident?"

"Yes," he said soberly. "It all happened so fast, knocked me for a loop. It took a long time to recover."

If you ever do.

"Maybe you never do," his words echoed my thoughts. "You just keep on living." He smiled pensively, drained his mug, and placed it on the table. "We should go." He grabbed the ticket as I reached for it.

"It's mine." He placed his warm hand over mine. I relented, and we stood up simultaneously. He scrutinized one side of my face.

"What is it?" I asked, patting my cheek.

"Nothing," he replied, with a sheepish grin.

"I'll meet you at the car." I scurried to the women's room. In the safety of the bathroom, I grimaced at my face and hair. I had just spent brunch sporting a mascara smudge under one eye and a piece of green pepper stuck between my front teeth. My ponytail scrunchie had slipped, and my hair was wild.

I repaired the damage and joined him, avoiding his amused expression. I slid into the passenger's seat. While he drove, I was off in another world, thinking about what he had said about his high school flame and Willow Rivers.

In the corridor, I unlocked my entrance, turned, and faced Don. He rested one hand on the doorjamb, bent over and kissed me. His soft lips brushed mine, and he murmured softly, "Thank you for brunch, Katelyn."

Next to my unit, Mrs. Gilman's doorknob rattled. She opened her entry and stepped out, startling us. "Oh hello, Katelyn." She sniffed.

Wayne's door opened at the end of the hall. "Yo," he greeted me. He nodded towards the sheriff, and asked, "Ready, Gillie?" She wore aqua hoodie and matching capris for the day's activity. Wayne wore new denim jeans and a blue plaid cotton shirt.

"Yes. Wayne, we'd better hurry if we're going to make the farmer's market," she trilled, fluffing her pixie hairdo. He grabbed her arm, and they strolled from the building.

Don grinned. "Cute couple."

"They are."

"I'll be going." He leaned over and pecked me on the forehead.

"Really?" I muttered after he left.

CHAPTER 20

I lost no time booting up my computer and Googling Willow Schmidt. Schmidt was a common name. Willow, not so much. I found John Schmidt at an address in Snake Hollow. I had tucked that bit away in my memory bank from my first conversation with Don. A person with an initial of 'W', along with two children, was listed with the man.

"That must be my lady," I said to Boots. If Willow wanted to remain anonymous, she should have moved away from her hometown.

She lived on the outskirts of town, with a county road address. I estimated it would take a couple of hours, round trip. I considered calling Eddy for the company, then decided against it. There was no telling what kind of mischief Eddy would get into. Wayne had just left with Gillie. I dialed Myra. Her phone went to voicemail, meaning she was busy. I hung up and printed out my Google map directions to supplement my GPS and grabbed my bag with Skye's journal.

I took the scenic old Highway 61 instead of the fast and furious interstate. It was a glorious June day, with fresh green grass and trees flush with new leaves. No sign of rain. I had blown my ninety-day goal for renovating the Hiptown project. I wanted to enjoy a day away from the snafus and solve the nagging problem of the bad karma by seeing Willow. I hoped to clear up the mystery of her photo in the house and see if she had any connection to Skye, even though she had denied everything to Don.

I flipped off the radio and reveled in the solitude and scenery of the drive. I didn't understand why Willow thought she could get lost in the country. People are more attuned to who fit in their community. They know everyone who lives there, and in many cases, their relatives before them.

Snake Hollow, population 384, sat at the top of a hill that intersected two winding county roads. The area appeared weary and forgotten. One had to question the wisdom of the settlers who named the village. It had three businesses; two were liquor establishments.

I stopped at a mom and pop convenience store/gas station. When I checked out with a diet cola, I showed the address to a robust thirty-something woman, with dark braided hair behind the counter. She immediately knew my destination, and said with a slightly broken accent, "Ya. Take the next road down, 'bout three miles in, number is on the mailbox." She looked me over, an unasked question lingering in her expression.

"Thank you."

She handed me change. She stared as if trying to gauge whether I was part of their hamlet. Dismissing me, "Ya betcha." She resumed watching out the window.

I grabbed my cola, got in my car, and surveyed the terrain. Taking the gravel road the woman had described, I navigated the wash-board terrain to the home that corresponded to the box number. I pulled into a long driveway that led to a two-story, white house with peeling paint.

I parked in the gravel driveway. I felt eyes on me as I trekked to the entry. The upstairs window curtains flipped, and a head ducked behind the window coverings.

I knocked. After a lengthy wait, during which I questioned my decision to come alone, and whether I should turn tail and run, a woman appeared in the doorway.

"Yes?" she asked. It was as if time had stood still. The youthful woman who stood before me had the same long brown hair tucked behind her ears and pensive face in the picture taken years earlier. Tall and lithe, she wore a blue and white patterned blouse with cut-off jean shorts.

"Hello." I cleared my throat. "My name is Katelyn Baxter. I'm renovating a home in Hiptown, where you once lived. I found your photo. I wonder if you could tell me anything about the place." She stepped out onto the wooden threshold and closed the door behind her.

"I told the police officer who called, I don't know why my picture was in the home," she said, with clear liquid brown eyes. "I never lived there. I did not know the dead girl. Please leave me be."

"I understand. I am sorry to bother you, but the renovation has been a nightmare, and anything you know about its history may help. Forgive me for intruding on your privacy, I understand you had problems, and you left an unhappy situation."

"Yes. I was clear with the officer I did not want to be found." She stood firm in her resolve. Her expression softened when I said, "I apologize. I would appreciate any help. Did you live in the Hiptown area?"

"No. I rented a room in a house by the university campus. I worked as a waitress to pay my rent. I was very young."

"Is there anybody you might have given this picture to?"

I dug into my purse and found a copy of the photo I had stashed.

"I must say, you haven't changed a bit." I unfolded the paper. "Do you remember who took the picture?"

She stiffened. Haltingly, "It was taken by a boy I knew at the diner where I worked. His name was Daemon. It became the poster photo for missing persons." She stared at the picture. "I came home after that summer. I searched for him at the restaurant later. The owner said he quit. He'd had an accident. Then, the papers were full of the news he had killed a girl who lived at the residence, Skye."

I dug the journal from my bag and held up the slim volume, with its butterfly cover in purple and pink, and the title "Dream."

"Do you recognize this?" I knew I was reaching, but had to try.

"No." She shook her head. "What is it?"

"Skye's journal. I discovered it in a window seat in a bedroom."

"No." She shrugged, brown eyes soft, a hint of something unsaid.

I waited. When she didn't respond, I returned the diary to my purse.

"Daemon Pleasant got off. He wasn't the killer. His landlord, Ruston Ahoe, confessed to the murder after they acquitted him. They released Daemon after Ruston confessed. Ruston could not be charged again because of the double jeopardy clause. No one can be tried twice for the same crime."

"Yes. I heard." She grimaced. Her hand trembled as she felt for the door handle.

Is she scared? As fast as the expression came, it vanished.

I heard the wail of a child from inside the house, and she said, “I have to go. My children need me.”

“I understand. Thank you for...”

She opened the entry, slipped inside, and shut the door in my face.

I drove back on the pitted gravel stretch, and out to the county road, my nerves unsettled, pondering my meeting with Willow. If Willow knew Daemon, who lived there, *why were Skye’s prints on the envelope that held Willow’s picture? They should have been Daemon’s prints.*

I took a detour to another part of the countryside, mulling over our conversation and enjoying the late afternoon’s lush scenery. My mind and body relaxed with the scent of evergreens and the beauty of the wild landscape. By the time I hit the old highway, I had unwound and anticipated more peace on the patio at my townhouse.

Boots greeted me with a yowl and tail held high when I blew in that night. I got his kibble, a snack for myself, and strolled to the patio to enjoy the quiet and balmy evening air. My peace was curtailed when I heard Mrs. Gilman and Wayne in the parking lot of the townhomes.

“But I didn’t want the cabbage. I wanted the carrots!” Mrs. Gilman protested. “Why don’t you listen to me?”

“I didn’t mean nothing, Gillie. I would have gotten the carrots, too,” Wayne said.

“I can’t eat both!”

“I’d help ya, Gillie,” Wayne came.

“That’s not the point! You never hear me,” Mrs. Gilman countered, her voice raised.

The argument continued until they were out of hearing range, Mrs. Gilman’s angst, and the handyman trying to soothe her ruffled feathers. I moved inside. I heard doors slamming, Gillie's, next to my home, and Wayne's, further down the hall.

"Looks like trouble in paradise, Boots." I shut my patio door.

The cat groomed his fur, jumped to his favorite resting place on the sofa, and curled up for the night.

CHAPTER 21

When I entered the renovation the next morning, Wayne was measuring off the damaged waterlogged bottom of the sheetrock from the broken water line. His face grim, he made pencil marks for the cuts.

"I have coffee and donuts!" I announced.

"Thanks." He grunted and made another mark.

"It's your favorite. Old-fashioned, chocolate-covered." I tried to cheer him up. The truth was, the donuts were my preferred snack. Wayne liked anything sugary. "No such thing as a bad carbohydrate," he would joke. He glanced at the bag and continued marking off the drywall.

"I'll put them over here." I wiped the dust from the counter and set the bag down. "What's the plan, Wayne?"

"Cut out the bad part of the sheetrock, put in a new piece, mud it, sand it down, and we'll be back in business."

"Sounds good." I shivered in the cold house, thinking about Saturday night's ghost busting adventure. I grabbed Skye's journal from my purse and marched to the second floor to check whether the rogue window was open in her old room. I breathed a sigh of relief, finding all the upstairs windows were securely closed. I tucked the journal inside the bench. I didn't want to misplace it.

Someone had to have snuck in while we were in the basement, messing with us. My bet would be on Eddy, except he was with the group the whole time. Randy and Misty's explanation that the open window could be an entrance for a ghostly presence was a little too convenient. For all I knew, they could have had someone open the windows to rattle us. If they had, it had worked, I was definitely on edge.

I considered my conversation with Willow yesterday, and the revelation that she knew Daemon Pleasant, aka Fast Freddie, from the restaurant where they both worked. Being nosy, I wanted to know Daemon's side of the story. Being frugal, I had not changed the latch on the back door the second time we found it open. Myra wasn't sure she had locked it.

With Ahoe sneaking out the kitchen exit, and the windows mysteriously open on the second level, it might be time to spend the big bucks with Fast Freddie and change the lock again.

I can't help being frugal. I would make a trip to Big Mart to get a new lock set and have the locksmith install it. I figured the store would have a better price on locks than Fast Freddie.

I left Wayne ripping out the bad portion of the drywall and headed over to the store. I snagged a lock and checked out, noting the cashier looked familiar. After I left the store, I realized it was the young man who had wanted the Bluebird house before I rented it to Eddy. I made a mental note, if anything happened with Eddy's rental, maybe the kid might qualify for a mortgage to buy it. You never know.

I hurried back to the renovation and called the locksmith from my car. He answered on the first ring. *Business must be slow.*

"Hey, Fast Freddie Locksmith here."

"Hi, Freddie, er Daemon. Do you mind if I call you Daemon?"

There was a lengthy pause, while he considered my voice. "Hey, no, this is Katelyn Baxter? Am I right?" he asked and chuckled.

"You are."

"How can I help?"

"I have a lock I'd like you to install at the rehab."

"Be there in about ten minutes," he responded.

"Perfect." I hung up, and entered through the front, past the construction mess. Wayne was in the kitchen, standing with his back against the counter. He swallowed the last morsel of a donut, licked the chocolate from his fingers, and said, "Thanks. I needed that." It was almost as if he'd had a drink.

"No problem." I paused, before asking, "Do you want to talk about it?"

"Who, Gillie? Naw, we're just taking a break." He crumpled the bag and threw it in the garbage.

"Sure." I nodded. "If you do, don't hesitate."

"Yep." We drifted to the patched drywall.

"By the way, I'm having Fast Freddie replace the deadbolt on the kitchen door."

"Heck. No need to pay him to install a lock. I can do that," he said.

"I know. You have enough to do, though. I want to talk to him."

"Huh?"

"About the envelope taped under the toilet tank."

"Thought the sheriff was checking that out?"

"He was, and he did. I took a little trip yesterday. The girl in the photo lives in a small burg up north. She knew Daemon Pleasant, also known as Fast Freddie."

"Fast Freddie is Daemon Pleasant?" His face creased, confused. He scratched his chin.

"Yes."

"Whoa, Kiddo." In the confusion of Eddy and Wayne dry walling, the ghost busting, and broken sink line, I'd forgotten to tell him who Fast Freddie was. "That's a whole different bag."

"Yes, it is. I am curious what he says about the photo. According to the sheriff, Skye's prints are on the envelope."

"Ya don't say?"

Just then, I saw Fast Freddie's truck drive up. I grabbed the bag with the new latch and hurried to meet him.

"Hey, Ms. Katelyn."

"Daemon." I waved him past the garage, to the back entry.

"You have a lock set?"

"Yes. I'm on a budget, and I picked one up at the store," I said, as an apology.

"Hey, no problem. I'll get to work."

I watched him install the new lock. After he finished, "Great, I'll get my purse." I grabbed my handbag, and met him at the back of his truck, where he was putting away tools.

I handed him my credit card.

"Daemon, I met a woman who said she knew you when you lived here with Ruston Ahoe." I dug out the photo of Willow stuffed in my purse. I held it up. He wiped his hands on his pants, took the picture, and peered at it, his eyes magnified behind eyeglass lenses. Slowly he returned the picture to me. "Willow. Where is she?"

"She doesn't want to be found," I said. "She's married with children and happy with her life."

"Hey," he drawled, "That's good. We were friends. That's all. She worked where I worked. We lost track of each other. Always wondered what happened to her." He shot me a dimpled smile.

"She said, she went back to the diner, and you had left. You'd had an accident?"

"Hey, yeah. Tried to outrun a train. Train won." He slammed the back doors to the van.

I stood still, mute, absorbing his words.

He went on, "Twisted my leg, snapped it in two places, getting out of the way. Stupid. Wasn't paying attention."

"Where was that?" I forced the question, my throat tight.

"Tracks over by Laguna," he said. "Hurt like hell." He faced me, "Hey, you look like you just saw a ghost."

Different train tracks.

I had an out-of-body experience; I observed Daemon closely. Minus the glasses and hat, he could be the same kid Jake had thrust to safety, losing his life in the process. But he wasn't.

Breathe.

"Sorry," I mumbled, collecting myself.

"Hey, can I get Willow's address?"

"She wants to be left alone. She married a guy by the name of John Schmidt and has children." Still numb, my heart beat wildly. I looked at the man with the dimpled smile and coke-bottle glasses in front of me. If he wanted to find Willow, he would have to do that on his own.

"Hey, that's okay, Ms. Katelyn. You know, Ruston played tricks on Skye."

"Tricks?" I snapped to attention. "What sort of tricks?"

"He had a player/recorder in the cellar. He programmed it to go off in the middle of the night."

"What?"

A veil flitted over Daemon's huge eyes as he talked. "He had creepy sounds recorded, a woman crying and objects thumping. The noises traveled up the vents to her room and would wake her. She went to the basement one night and discovered the machine. She was furious."

"She confronted Ahoe?"

"She tried. She told me the next day, she had ripped out the player and banged on his door, but he wouldn't answer. She smashed the device and left it outside his door. I was working the overnight shift at the diner when it happened."

"He was a coward."

"Hey, yeah," he said. "Next thing I knew, Ruston said she moved out."

"So, he must have killed her soon after she found the recorder?" I hazarded a guess and shuddered.

"Hey, maybe."

"Why would Ahoe torment her?"

"He wanted her."

"What do you mean?" I asked, grimly.

"He wanted her to like him."

My stomach curdled.

"He did that stuff so she would come running to him. He would be the hero and rescue her. When she discovered the player, it backfired. She wanted nothing to do with him."

"Ruston's logic was twisted."

"Evil," he said. "Hey, thanks for telling me about Willow. Glad she's okay." He grasped my hand for a shake and dropped it. His touch was icy. "I owe you one." He smiled a wide toothy smile, flashed his dimples, got into the company truck, and sped away.

I stood on the sidewalk and stared at the departing truck. I could not believe another kid had met the same fate on railroad tracks, just as the kid Jake saved. I hadn't asked a lot of questions. But the enormity of what Daemon had said about his accident stirred a flood of emotions.

I spent the rest of the day helping Wayne with the drywall. We got the taping, and first coat of mud applied. It would take two or three coats of mud and sanding to get the seams smooth.

Later, at home, grungy and weary, I gave Boots a treat and headed to the bathroom, stripped, and showered. Wrapping my head with a towel and slipping on a robe, I went to the kitchen to find dinner.

I was studying the dismal prospects inside the fridge.

"Yo. Wifey," came the voice behind me.

"Eddy!" I raised my head, hitting the edge of the refrigerator. "Don't do that! Why are you here?" I backed out, whirled around, and faced him. "How did you get in?"

"You gave me a key."

"Oh, yes. I forgot. You're supposed to call first," I countered. I had let him keep the key after he moved into the Bluebird place. In case of an emergency, I could call him if I needed anything from home. Not the brightest thing I've ever done.

"Then, I wouldn't need a key. You're cute," he said, leering at me. Leaning over, he kissed me on the forehead.

"Why are you here?" My eyes narrowed.

"I was in the neighborhood, thought I'd stop in," he said. "How about I take you out for dinner?"

"You still have a job?" I grilled him, concerned about the Bluebird rent coming due. He had said the company had rehired him. I hoped that bit of wonderful news hadn't changed.

"Yep." He laughed.

"I'll get dressed."

We were seated at Popov's later that night at a table by the dance floor.

"So, you dropped by to take me out to dinner?"

Eddy sat back, took a sip of Happy Hour ale, and offered me a taste. I sipped the drink. It had a decidedly lime flavor, and my mouth puckered.

"Maybe," he submitted.

"Okay? What is it?"

"Katelyn, the Bluebird house needs a family. It's too much for a bachelor, like me."

My stomach did a dive. "So, what are you thinking, Eddy?"

"Kate, let's get married."

Nooooooo.

Although the word had not come out, the shock registered on my face. He looked away with a fleeting expression of hurt. I protested, "You can't be serious. We fought all the time when we were married."

"We were kids back then. Think about it, Kate. That's all I ask." He stretched his long legs out and watched raptly as Popov's set up for the evening karaoke event.

The server brought our food, and I said, "I'll have a glass of wine."

"Six ounces or nine ounces?"

"Nine ounces. Better make that two nine-ounce glasses."

It was going to be a long night.

CHAPTER 22

"Yo. How you doing this fine morning?" Wayne greeted me the next day at the Hiptown house.

"You're in a good mood." *Had he seen Eddy's truck parked at the townhouse last night?*

"Yep, Gillie and I have an understanding."

"Oh?" I said, relieved. I did not want to explain Eddy. I was still in shock. Numbed by a lot of wine last night and a headache today.

As Wayne explained, my cell rang. I reached for the phone. He waved and said, "Later." He started up the sander to smooth the compound on the drywall tape.

"Thanks," I mouthed and answered. It was Myra. I stepped outside to the porch to talk while the sander roared.

"Hi."

"Are you okay?" she asked.

"I've been better," I admitted. "It's Eddy."

"How about lunch?" she suggested, "Popov's. One o'clock?"

"I'll be there."

I gestured towards Wayne, and he turned off the machine.

"What did you and Gillie decide?"

He put the sander down. "We're going to counseling."

"Really?" My eyebrows rose. "That's very mature."

"Yep. She's going to Al-Anon. I'm sticking to AA."

"I thought it was just family members who belonged to Al-Anon? Don't couples go together for therapy? How will that help?"

"No. Friends can go to Al-Anon. Gillie's more than a friend; she is pretty near family. She can talk stuff out with Al-anon people. I'll talk it out in AA."

"And what about the two of you counseling together?"

"Haven't got that far. It ain't perfect. Nothing is."

"That's true. You'll work it out." I added, "It's a great start."

"Yep." He nodded confidently and started sanding.

"Good customer!" Ivan said as I entered Popov's. The cranky manager showed me to a booth where Myra waited for me. She looked fresh. I wore my work shirt and had taken a swipe at my face in the car, wiping off drywall dust, and combing my hair.

After we ordered, she leaned in and asked in a low tone, "What's up with Eddy?"

"He wants to get married."

"Noooooo," she said and groaned.

"My reaction, exactly."

"What are you going to do?"

"Don't know." I shrugged. "Been there, done that."

Our food came, and I bit into the big burger, savoring the flavors of the special sauce, cheese, and beef.

"A lot has happened since the ghost busting," I said.

"What?"

"After Wayne and I cleaned the yard from the storm debris, Don asked me to brunch."

"You have been busy." She smiled. "He's such a nice man."

"Yes." I sighed. "He said that Willow Rivers was now Mrs. John Schmidt. I drove to Snake Hollow where she lives."

"Really? Don gave you her address?"

"No. I Googled it. He had told me her family was from Snake Hollow. Took a chance she returned home and married the one John Schmidt in the burg."

"Okay." She sipped her coffee and leaned back. "Everything's online, now." She sniffed, resigned.

"Willow said she and Daemon worked at the same cafe. Later, she tried to find him at the diner. But he wasn't there."

Myra pushed her plate away and nodded. "Go on."

"He'd had an accident. He broke his leg, outrunning a train," I said.

"Not Jake...?"

I shook my head. "Different tracks."

"Okay." Myra nodded, relieved.

"She said she didn't know why her photo was in Ahoe's old house. She didn't know Skye."

"It's possible that Daemon had Willow's photo. Skye found it and taped it under the tank?"

"That's possible." Puzzled, I asked, "Why?"

"Maybe it was some sort of warning? Or stress because of Ruston?"

"Maybe?" I finished my burger, put my plate aside, and took a gulp of coffee. Just then, I caught sight of a couple following the touchy hostess. Myra followed my gaze, and we exchanged glances.

It was Don Williams. The silver in his blond hair sparkled. He was out of uniform, and his broad shoulders filled out a blue chambray shirt. He smiled down at the petite redhead at his side and waited until the elfin-faced nymph eased into a booth. He slid in beside her, his back to Myra and me.

When does this guy work?

I drained my coffee mug and reached for my handbag on the bench seat beside me. "I have to go."

"It could be nothing," Myra said. "Could be his sister?"

"Sitting on the same side of the booth? Don't know. Don't care." I left some bills on the table. "I have to go." Then, I got up and strolled over to where Don and the woman sat, heads huddled together, talking. I stopped at their booth. With a big smile, I fluttered my eyelashes, leaned over, and let my purse hit the glass of water in front of him. It fell over. Redheaded nymph jumped out of the way. The water and glass hit his man parts, and he shot up.

"Sorry," I said with a backward glance.

Myra followed me from the restaurant. I left her at her SUV, speechless.

I trotted to my car with the lyrics of a classic country song by Dottie West, "A Lesson in Leavin'" ...running through my mind.

CHAPTER 23

My energy level was heightened by my angst, and I doubled down on getting the renovation done. It showed, and the place looked good.

It had been two weeks since I had seen Don and the elfin-faced woman at Popov's.

Any troublesome happenings had ceased, and I was satisfied that whatever, or whomever, had haunted the house was gone. Either by the ghost busting or by the fact Ruston Ahoe was in jail. I was painting the newly redesigned, open concept room after finishing the floors, and painting the two bedrooms and hall on the second floor. Wayne had finished the first-floor bathroom and was working on the upstairs main bath.

While I painted, a breeze filtered through the ajar door and open windows, airing out the space. Distracted by Fast Freddie's Locksmith truck parked behind my car on the street, I stopped and peered. His back doors were open, obstructing my view of the front bumper of the vehicle. I put down my paint roller and watched. *Daemon spends a lot of time fixing locks in this neighborhood.*

A squad car pulled up and parked in front of Fast Freddie's van.

It couldn't be.

Rap. Rap.

I answered the knock, my nerves on alert. Don was in uniform, and his broad shoulders filled the front door frame.

"Lately, I haven't seen much of you, Kate." He cleared his throat. "I wanted to tell you something."

"What?" I nursed an attitude from the last time I'd seen him at the restaurant.

"The woman you spoke with at Snake Hollow wasn't Willow."

"How do you know about my visit?" I asked.

"She called and complained. She said she had a visitor, a woman who identified herself as Katelyn Baxter."

"Oh." I winced.

"I told you she didn't want to be located. How did that happen?"

"I took a stab that the John Schmidt in Snake Hollow was the same fellow who married Willow. The woman who appeared at the door looked just like the photograph. She didn't say she *wasn't* Willow." I was on the defensive, and he knew it.

"Katelyn," his voice was patient and deliberate. "She resembles Willow because she's her younger sister, Winona. Could be a twin, near as I can tell from her license photo."

"So, Willow is still missing?"

"It appears so."

"Why didn't you know she was a sister, when we had breakfast?" I demanded.

"She was cagey on the phone. Paranoid, even. Wouldn't say she was not Willow. She sounded scared, which got me thinking, and I did more digging. But that is my job, not yours. Are we clear, Katelyn?" His eyes fixed on my face.

"Yes. I'm sorry. I shouldn't have snooped." I avoided his gaze, one hand behind my back, fingers crossed.

"You'd be correct about that. Anything else?"

"There is something I want to ask," I took a deep breath.

"Yes?"

I cleared my throat, "Who were you with at Popov's?" I stared at him. "You had company. A little redhead."

"You mean when you dumped a glass of ice water in my lap?"

"Oh, yeah. That." I flinched again.

He considered me with a slight grin, and his manner changed. "Nice to know you care." He walked out.

What does that mean?

Wayne descended the stairs, carrying the base of the old toilet from the second-floor bath and interrupted my musing.

"I'll get the door," I said, and hurried to open the front entry. He deposited the fixture in the dumpster. He came back, rubbing his hands. "Heavy sucker. They don't make 'em like that anymore. One more piece." He took the staircase two steps at a time, stretching his lanky legs. He emerged with the tank. I met him at the exit again, holding it for another trip to the dumpster. The sheriff's vehicle, along with the locksmith's van, had left.

"Guess I'll get some lunch." Wayne nodded at me.

"Sounds good. I have a sandwich. I'll finish painting."

"I'll grab a hotdog. Be back to put in the toilet."

"Good. The range and refrigerator are being delivered this afternoon," I said, viewing the kitchen.

"Great."

I took a breath, savoring the results. "It is a great renovation. Don't you think?"

"It is. Better, now that the danged ghost has vanished."

"I guess whatever the paranormal investigators did, it worked," I agreed.

"Haven't had a door slam or a window open on its own. Been decent," he said. "Haven't seen another mouse, either."

"Life is good," I agreed with a laugh.

"Sure 'nuff is," Wayne said and chuckled.

After he left, I painted and thought about my conversation with Don. Had Willow's family given up on trying to find her? Why did her sister, Winona, let me believe she was Willow? It made little sense. Wouldn't she want to know what happened to her sister? Did she *know* where her sister was? Winona appeared scared and pleaded to remain anonymous. Both Don and I agreed on that point. What *had* happened to Willow?

The arrival of the kitchen appliances interrupted my pondering. The delivery people from the home store rolled the fridge into place and plugged it in. Easy breezy, ready to go. They carted in the new range, removing the old.

"The plumber has to come and finish hooking up the gas stove," one young man said. "I'll call, let him know it's here."

"Thank you."

Wayne came back from lunch. From the crumbs on his shirt, I suspected he had eaten a donut for dessert. He hoisted a new toilet up the stairs and installed the fixture while I continued painting.

The plumber arrived and hooked up the range, putting a safety valve on the line, explained the digital dials, and left the paperwork.

"Gas, huh?" Wayne asked. We were viewing the bright shiny appliances.

"I decided to replace what was there," I said "I like gas. It'll help sell the house, too."

"They sure are pretty." He whistled.

"They are," I agreed. Late afternoon, I toured the home, admiring the new fixtures in the upstairs bath, the kitchen appliances, and the paint job. "It's been a full day. Let's call it quits. You go ahead. I'll lock up."

"You got it." He took off. I lingered, quickly swept the kitchen, cleared the central living area of painting supplies, and latched the windows.

Ready to leave, I hesitated and detoured to the basement. I viewed the area. Shrugging at the gloomy space. *It would always be just a creepy basement*. It was cold and dank. That would be next week's job, repairing the chipped cement by the storage room. Dusting, painting, cleaning. I had my work cut out with trying to brighten the cellar. I trekked upstairs, grabbed my purse, locked the doors, and headed out.

"Dang it!" I groaned and twisted the key in my Ford. Nothing. The car refused to start. It had been blissfully reliable for 'cheap, used.' I tried the key again. Silence. I got out and checked under the hood.

"What in the world?" I gawked at the space where a battery should have been. No battery. Gone. MIA. Tired and unkempt, I considered my options: Call Eddy, whom I had been ducking since he proposed. Call the sheriff, when he'd left on a baffling note. Wayne? I hated to contact him after all the work he had done that day. Myra won out.

"Hi, you wouldn't be able to take me to an auto supply store for a car battery, would you? I'm at the Hiptown rehab."

"Your battery died?" she guessed. She was well acquainted with my economy cars.

"Not exactly."

She waited.

"Someone stole the battery."

"You're kidding."

"Myra, I would not kid about an MIA battery."

"I'm on my way."

I left the hood of my Ford up so she could see I wasn't joking. Within ten minutes, she arrived, parking behind the disabled automobile. She stepped out of her vehicle and met me at the front.

"Yikes." She peered at the vacant space in the engine block. "That's a new one," she laughed. "Let's get you a battery."

KABOOOOOM!

Stunned by the sounds of an explosion, we ducked while shingles and pieces of wood and stucco rained down, littering the lawn and the car.

Myra fell against me, and we hit the ground. Disoriented, I blinked at a world flipped upside down. I eased out from under her body, quickly brushed off rubble, and twisted, rising to my knees. I looked down at her, tossing aside pieces of litter.

"Myra. Myra?" I pleaded, my heart pounding. She opened her eyes and blinked. I asked, "Are you okay? Can you hear me?" In the distance, I heard the sirens of emergency rescue vehicles.

She stared at me blankly, then reality dawned, and she asked, "What happened?"

"The house exploded." I let out a breath of relief. Myra was all right.

Groaning, she sat up. "Well, that's one hell of a deal." It was the one time in the dozen years I'd known her that I heard her curse.

"Don't rush," I said. She gingerly felt her arms and stretched her legs.

"I'm okay." By then, the dwelling was on fire, and orange-red flames shot from the kitchen exit.

I stood up and helped her to her feet. Suddenly, I counted four fire trucks, several squad cars, and an ambulance. Police officers marshaled us across the street, away from the inferno. As we watched, the firefighters put out the blaze that lit up the sky. My mind and body were in shock as the fruits of my labor burned.

"Katelyn!" It was Don. His hand rested on my shoulder, "Are you all right?" I nodded numbly. He turned to Myra. "How are you?"

Myra nodded, stunned. She put her arm around my shoulders and told me what I already knew. "Kate, the police will want to talk to you. There will be an investigation. They have to find out how this happened."

"I don't know what happened. When I left, everything was fine. I came out. The car wouldn't start. The battery was gone." I blithered and shook my head. "Stolen."

"They still need to take your report," she said.

"Yes," Don said. "You can ride with me to the station. You're positive you aren't hurt?"

"I'm good," I replied.

"We're fine, Sheriff," Myra said. "I'll come, too."

CHAPTER 24

"More wine?" Myra asked. It was close to midnight by the time we finished with the police. She insisted I come home with her after making the report. I showered at her house, and she lent me a new pair of pajamas. They were a beautiful set of silk designer duds, luxurious. I could get used to this.

"Fill 'er up," I said, holding up a crystal wine glass.

Next, I dialed Wayne, "Sorry I'm calling so late. Can you let yourself into my townhouse and feed Boots? There is a situation at the rehab. I'll fill you in tomorrow." I didn't have the heart to tell him about the explosion.

"Sure, Kiddo. No problem." He hung up. I joined Myra in her family room facing the lake. The full moon and brilliant stars lit up the sky as we each cradled a glass of wine, lost in our thoughts, gazing at the night sky.

"At least you are insured," Myra said.

"It burned to the freaking ground. Skye's diary was there, too." I groaned. "I placed it inside the window seat after my visit with Willow, or Winona, as it turns out."

"Did the sheriff ever find Skye's family?"

"I don't think so. He said they left the city after the verdict." I shrugged.

"Maybe it's a sign."

"A sign?"

"The diary is where it should be. It could have been a painful memory for the family." Myra's expression was thoughtful.

"Yes, you're right. The house blowing up is a blessing. It puts an end to all the bad karma."

"And insurance will help you rebuild. It'll be a new home, free of spirits haunting the dwelling."

"They'll have to dig out the foundation and dispose of everything," I added.

"Yes. They will."

"It must have been the stove," I speculated. "Something had to have gone wrong with the gas connection?"

"Maybe. The police will investigate. The fire inspector will determine the cause of the explosion," she said.

"Myra, I'm a Home Rehab Specialist. I'm not a new home builder," I protested.

"Are you saying you don't want to rebuild on the lot?"

"Yep." I nodded and sipped my wine.

"Hmmm, you don't think you might change?" she added, "New is nice."

"Don't want to change." I shook my head. "I like fixing things."

Myra looked at me as if I'd lost my mind. "You should get some rest. It has been a long day."

While I slept, Myra threw my work clothes into the washer and dryer, and they were ready in the morning. I reluctantly left the silk jammies on the bed. The following day was Saturday. She drove me to the auto supply store to get a battery for my car.

The Hiptown house was a pile of rubble. We stood for a moment, staring at the crime scene tape that cordoned off the lot from passersby. Both of us unconsciously made the sign of the cross as we examined the devastation.

My trusty Ford Festiva was covered in dust and debris. I cleared it off with a bench brush and a Minnesota staple—a long-handled snow brush that stayed in the car during every season.

"Think it'll start with a new battery?" I asked her.

"We won't know until we try. Let's get out of here." I hopped into Myra's SUV, and we sped to the nearest auto parts store.

I told the clerk at the auto store what had happened.

"You're kidding," he said.

"I would not kid about an MIA battery," I said, for the second time in as many days. I felt my face flush, and my shoulders tense.

The clerk did his best to keep a smirk under control as he explained how to hook up the battery. "If you have any problems, call. I'll have my parts runner meet you, and he can install it."

"That would be great." I handed over my credit card, mentally calculating the available balance. I relaxed when the card was approved.

I took the battery, and Myra and I headed to the Ford. I popped in the part and connected the cables. I tried the ignition, and the car roared to life. I was back in business. I gave a thumbs up sign to Myra. She drove away. I waited a few minutes for the battery to charge, then I motored off, trying to avoid staring at the pile of destruction that was my home renovation.

"Yowl! Yowl!" Boots was furious when I blew in. I couldn't blame him. I gave him extra kibble, petted him, and fell into bed. I wanted to block out the entire episode.

Sunday, I wakened to the telephone.

"Wifey?"

"Eddy, I can't marry you again."

"It's okay," He said in a low voice, "I heard about the home explosion. I had to be sure you were all right."

"Thanks, Eddy, I'm fine. I'm sleeping." I hung up.

Later that day, Myra called. "How are you feeling?"

"Fine."

"That good?"

"Yep."

"I was curious, so I called my brother," she said, hesitating. "He talked to an investigator at the Hiptown police station and got the inside scoop. He said the inspector found something."

"What?" I asked, puzzled.

"They found the body of a man in the rubble. They think he was killed during the explosion."

"Someone was inside when it exploded?"

"Yes."

"OMG! Who?"

"They don't have an identification yet. I thought you would like to know. There's something else, Katelyn."

"What?" I demanded.

"They found a skull. In the ruins of the house."

"OMG! Good grief!"

I started a pot of java and rattled around my townhouse, straightening, cleaning, and gathering my wits. I had been lax about cleaning while getting the Hiptown renovation in order. I hung pictures in the living room. It was a small thing. Puttering at home has always had a calming effect. Some people take bubble baths or do yoga. I paint, rearrange furniture, photos, or scout out dwellings for rehab.

Later that night, with a hammer in hand, I stood back admiring my progress.

KNOCK. KNOCK.

I checked the peephole and saw the profile of Fast Freddie, aka Daemon Pleasant. He heard me, pivoted, and blinked. I opened the door to the boyish-faced man with a wide dimpled smile and enormous eyes.

"Hey, Ms. Katelyn,"

"Hi, Daemon. What are you doing here?"

Boots hopped down from the sofa, weaved between my legs, glared up at the man and yowled.

"I was worried. I saw the place was wrecked. I had to check on you. Hey, I hope that's okay." His big smile engaging, his arms open, hands spread in a pleading gesture.

"How did you find me?" I asked. I examined him, hesitating. I held the hammer, poised to hang more pictures.

"I Googled you. Hey, you can find anybody, anywhere." He chuckled. Mrs. Gilman opened her door. I had not talked to Wayne about the renovation and hoped he hadn't seen or heard anything on the news. I hated to tell him all our hard work was for naught, never mind what Myra said about the inspector finding a dead man, or a skull. I was still absorbing the news myself.

"Hey, can I come in? I have info about the house." He glanced at Mrs. Gilman.

Boots hissed at Daemon, tail high, and leaped to his perch on the sofa, watching.

"Sure." I let him in. I waved him to the kitchen table and put the hammer on the counter. "Have a seat."

He limped to the table and sat, shifting in the chair. He wiped at his brow with his shirtsleeve.

"I have coffee. Would you like a cup? Just made it. It's Colombian, strong stuff," I warned.

"Hey, I don't want to put you out."

"No. You're not. Coffee is always on," I said. My back to him, I reached for a mug from the cupboard and filled it. "What did you hear about the renovation? I heard they found a body in the rubble."

"Yeah. It's Ruston Ahoe."

I paused, and a chill traveled my spine. *How does he know that?*

"I thought he was in jail?"

"His mom bailed him out."

"Oh." I stopped filling the cup. I carefully replaced the carafe. I twisted and faced him. "You seem to know a lot about the neighborhood. I wouldn't think you'd be buddies with Ruston after doing time for a murder he did?"

"Hey, he got me sprung. He confessed. 'Quid pro quo!'" He gave a low, hard laugh. The hair on the back of my neck stood up. The air in the kitchen became thick with tension. I placed my hand close to the hammer on the counter.

"What do you mean?"

"It's what Rusty used to say, 'quid pro quo. I do your job, you do mine.' He was smart."

"What do you mean?"

"Hey, back in the day, in high school," Daemon said, a wide grin on his face, "I did stuff for Rusty, and he did favors for me. We were never together, so we didn't get caught. It was a kick!" He chortled.

"What kind of stuff?" I inhaled and listened.

"One time they kicked me out of school for smoking dope in the boy's room, Rusty painted the principal's house with cuss words in red. The principal tried to pin it on me, but he couldn't. I was working that crummy diner job."

"What did you do for Rusty?" My heart pounded.

"I slashed the coach's tires. Put sugar in his gas tank. What a kick!"

"Why?"

"Rusty snuck into the girl's locker room and planted a recorder. He played the show in the boy's restroom. Coach walked in and busted him. He wasn't *that* smart."

He laughed again. “He got caught. They suspended him.”

“How did you meet Ruston if you didn’t hang out in school?”

“We hooked up at the diner. He came in one day, all bummed out, and recognized me. We started kidding around. Started making deals.”

“Skye and Willow worked at the same restaurant?”

“We were the three musketeers.” He laughed. “‘til Rusty got ahold of Willow.”

“What happened?” I inhaled, uneasy. Dread filled me.

“He showed up one night at the cafe. He left right after Willow’s shift. She never worked at the cafe again.”

“Skye said she thought Rusty did something to Willow?” I guessed.

“I told her she was crazy. She called the cops.”

“That was the 9-1-1 call?”

“Yeah. They couldn’t nail Rusty for Willow, cuz nobody saw them together. It was cold and rainy that night. But, at the trial for Skye’s murder, they had a recording of me yelling at her. An ‘incident.’” He chuckled and sneered, “Nobody was out, business was slow and the owner sent Willow home early. But the 9-1-1 call busted me for Skye.”

“But she backed down, and the cops left. And they didn’t know about Willow?” I asked.

“Yeah. Skye liked me. She didn’t want me to get hauled off to jail.”

“Okay?” My shoulders tensed and I asked. “Do you still play pranks?”

“Like open windows and slam doors?” he chortled.

“It was you and Ruston, the night of the paranormal investigators?”

“It was too good, man. The guy had a van with a logo and everything.”

"The doorknob?"

"Yep."

"The sounds like a cat crying?"

"Must have been Ruston and his recorder. He loved that stuff."

"But why pull pranks on me?"

"You bought the place. Ruston wanted the house. It was *his.*"

"You killed Skye?" I glanced at Daemon, my hand within an inch of the tool.

"Yep." He chortled. "You got me."

"Ahoe killed Willow? It's her skull? That's why he confessed after they acquitted him of Skye's murder. He knew you would squeal on him if you rotted in jail when he got off. You had evidence that could jail him for thirty years. You knew where her body was. No one, except you and Ruston, knew about Willow until Skye found out. You forced Skye to tape Willow's picture under the tank lid, then murdered her. If you were caught, you would blow the whistle on Ruston about Willow's murder. Skye knew Ahoe killed her!"

"She guessed. She was on to Ruston's tricks. She kept that damned diary. It was there somewhere."

"That's right. You asked me about the window seat." I watched him closely as my mind flashed to the question that seemed odd when Daemon said he had lived in the house.

"I thought it might be there."

I took a deep breath. "Yes. It was under a false bottom. But there wasn't anything in it. In fact, she said she liked you."

"Is that so?" he asked.

Daemon's demeanor turned black. His owl-like eyes glared at me through thick lenses. He lunged out of the chair, upending it, and rushed for the hammer, twisting it out of my reach. With my other hand, I grabbed the carafe of coffee and pitched the glass container at his face.

"Aaaaaah," he screamed. The hot liquid coursed down his face, seeping behind his eyeglasses. The carafe bounced off his forehead and broke into pieces behind him. He closed his eyes, swiping at the scorching liquid. I lunged for the hammer, wrenching it from his grasp.

"Why did you do it? Why did you kill Skye?" I yelled, brandishing the tool.

"I didn't want to, but Rusty killed Willow first. I did it for him. Skye was ready to squeal. Quid pro quo."

"Did you go to Snake Hollow to threaten Winona?" I screamed. "Is that why she doesn't want anyone to know where she is?"

"The owner of the diner told me Willow's sister was looking for her. Said the sister was a dead ringer for Willow. Willow told her about me."

"After Willow disappeared, and Skye turned up dead, Winona put it together. It scared her when you both got out of jail. She was afraid she might be next. She couldn't prove anything." I sputtered at Daemon. I hit him on his bad leg with the hammer, my breath coming in spurts. "You were playing tricks, the noises, the open windows."

"You bitch! You're supposed to be dead!"

"What does that mean? You animal!" I lifted the hammer, poised to use it.

"I stole your battery right under that cop's nose."

"Huh?" I remembered the day Don came to the rehab. Fast Freddie's van had been parked in front of my car; the back-panel doors open. I stared at Daemon.

"Yeah. You were supposed to go into the house and die with Rusty. But he could never do nothing right. He turned the stove burners on and waited for you. But you didn't go back. You waited outside for that lady."

"Myra."

"It was the perfect time to get rid of Rusty. I lit a match and tossed it into the kitchen, locked the door, and ran like hell. He never saw it coming. It took a few seconds and bam!" He chortled.

"Why d'you kill Ahoe?" I yelled, holding the hammer high.

"I did time for him!"

"But you murdered Skye. Ahoe killed Willow. Quid pro quo."

"Only counts if you don't get caught! I got jail time. Rusty didn't. He laughed at me. He thought he was so smart! He's dead now."

I popped him again on his kneecap. He fell to the floor screaming. Howling in pain, he screamed, "It wasn't just me doing tricks. It was Rusty, too!" He rose, his pain and anger giving him strength.

I dived for his other leg. He shoved me. I fell back, maintaining a grip on the hammer. "Where is Willow's body? Where?" Gasping, I regained my balance, brandishing the weapon. I slammed his good leg with the tool.

He screamed, coiled, and grabbed at my legs. I twisted away, kicking his hands, wielding the tool. I bopped him on the side of his head with the flat side of the hammer's head. He toppled over on his side, howling, his hands clutching his head and his glasses flying across the room.

"Tell me, or I'll do it again!"

"She was in the canning room," he gasped. "Next to the stairwell. Now. Stop!"

I blinked. "Where the cement surface was flaking?"

"Yeah. Cops missed it."

I kicked him.

"Aaaaaah!"

"That's for doing a crummy job curing the cement, you bastard!"

The cat leaped from the sofa, a blur of black and white fur, claws extended.

"Owwee! Get it off me!" Daemon rolled on the floor in pain, fighting to get the cat from his back. Boots hung on for dear life, biting and snarling.

"Police! Open up!" My door burst open. Don charged in, another officer behind him. Mrs. Gilman and Wayne waited outside my door, watching, their eyes wide.

"Katelyn, I'll take it from here," Sheriff Don said. "Get ahold of Boots," he ordered.

I grabbed the cat from Daemon's back and yelled, "Not so fast! How did you hurt your leg? Why do you limp?"

Daemon was face down on the floor as Sheriff Don cuffed his wrists behind his back.

"I tripped," he whined. "Running."

"Why were you running?" I demanded.

Daemon mumbled something under his breath. I leaned down. "I can't hear you!"

"I held up a seven-eleven. Now get that cat away from me!" I kept my grip on Boots as I grilled Daemon. "You knew about Jake and how he died, you slime ball! You wanted to get my sympathy!" I held the cat twisting in my arms, next to Daemon's head.

"Everything's online! Take the damn cat!"

The sheriff jerked Daemon to his feet, and he and his deputy removed him to the police car.

"I'll be back to take your report, Katelyn," Sheriff Don said over his shoulder.

"Kiddo, are you, all right?" Wayne and Mrs. Gilman stood back while the officers carted Daemon away. Wayne's hand was on Mrs. Gilman's shoulder, her eyes were as large as saucers. She said, "Katelyn, we heard the ruckus and called 9-1-1. Whatever happened?"

"That was Fast Freddie? The locksmith?" Wayne asked. "What was he doing here?"

"Yes. Wayne, please sit down. You, too, Gillie." With a questioning glance at each other, they sat on the sofa, waiting.

"The renovation is pretty much toast," I said, "There was an explosion and it's a total loss."

"Oh, my word," Gillie said.

"It's for the best. That place never did feel right," he said.

"You always complained it was haunted, Wayne," Mrs. Gilman said, gazing adoringly at the handyman. "I'm positive you were correct." He glowed at her compliment.

That counseling must be working.

CHAPTER 25

I cooled my heels in the waiting area outside of the sheriff's office. Because they arrested Daemon in my townhouse in Crocus Heights, it was in Don's jurisdiction, and he was taking my report.

"I heard you yell something about Willow before we burst in. What was that about?"

"Daemon knew Willow had a sister. Winona, and she was hiding from him," I said. "He found her and threatened her."

"How did Daemon find her?"

Yikes, how am I going to get out of this?

"I may have let a name slip," I muttered. "You can Google anything now." I avoided his gaze. He leaned back in his chair and studied me. He sat up, tossed the report aside, and abruptly spoke, "Yes. I guess you can."

"So, I'm done, right?" I stood up. He stood up. The air filled with unasked questions and I waited, scrutinizing his broad shoulders, his silvery-blond hair.

"I have a question," I said, and took a deep breath.

"Yes?"

I cleared my throat. "What did you mean about my dumping water on you, showed I cared?"

While I stared at him, his manner became distant.

"Katelyn, I think it's best we're friends." He cleared his throat, looked back at the paper on his desk. Anywhere besides my face.

My face flushed the color of a beet. I walked out of his office, the lyrics of "Crash and Burn" by Thomas Rhett running through my mind. Another love crashed and burned.

I called Myra when I got home. "You wouldn't want to come over tonight?"

"I could."

"You wouldn't have any wine, would you?"

"I do."

"How about a lavender-scented candle?"

"Oh, oh. I suppose you want sage?" At my Bluebird rehab, we had done a sage burning to cleanse the house of any bad karma from the dead body I had found during the renovation. She wasn't a fan of the ritual, but she tolerated my quirks. The Hiptown rehab had triggered her own superstitions.

"Wouldn't hurt."

"I'll bring sage," her voice quiet.

While I waited for Myra. I pulled the boxes from my bedroom closet that I had packed away after Jake died. I started sorting through them. I threw clothes into donation boxes and tossed old files. I took out photos I had kept and tucked the best picture of us on built-in shelves in the living room. I put out a vase and souvenir mugs from our years together. I had cleared the last box out by the time she knocked.

I let her in and motioned her to the bedroom.

"You've been busy." She observed the piles. "Where is all this stuff going?"

"Out. I'll be a few minutes."

"I'll get the wine and light the candle."

"Don't light the herb bundle without me."

"Never," she said, getting out stemware.

I hustled boxes out of the house, first to the dumpster, then toted the donation boxes to the car.

When I finished, Myra handed me a glass of white wine. We headed to the couch and sat. Boots settled on the sofa back.

"Tough day?" She asked.

"Yep." I sipped my vino. "I took a page from Wayne's book and decided to be honest and ask the sheriff what he meant about the cold-water dump."

"And?"

"He said he thought it was best we were friends. He stammered when he said it."

"Ah." She had a sip of wine, and conceded, "He is single. There is single, engaged, or married. No going steady. He can have friends. You could be a friend." She shrugged; her expression thoughtful.

"Yes." I nodded and gulped the chardonnay. "I got ahead of myself."

"Don't be too hard on yourself. It is his loss. Friends." She sniffed.

"Thanks, Myra." I nodded, emptying my glass, placing it on the coffee table. "Let's burn some sage."

We settled in the living area after the last bit of the sage bundle had burned.

"I'm prepared to buy the Hiptown place. *If*, you're positive about not wanting to build." She waited, expectantly.

"Are you sure, Myra?" I was surprised. "Do you really want to buy that house?"

"It wouldn't be the same dwelling. It would be a new home. A fresh beginning for the land," she said, fingering the rim of her glass, pensive. "I think it would be a splendid way to cleanse the spot and renew it for new occupants."

"It would," I admitted. "It has a kind of symmetry. A fresh start for a new occupant. The spirits from Willow Rivers and Skye Jones satisfied by Ruston Ahoe's death and Daemon in jail. Finally, some justice for the women."

"Not to mention, it would give peace to my mother's lover and child." She added, "The man who might have been my father." Her expression was heavy, then she brightened. "It would banish any spirits. They would have to leave, there would be no connection to the dwellings. They would be gone."

"Um," I said, and fingered my glass. "I don't think that's necessarily true, if the spirits are connected to the land. But it seems the only spirits there were at the pleasure of Ruston Ahoe and his mischief with recorders."

"And, Daemon with his ability to get in and out of houses. He blended in with the neighborhood. Nobody ever questioned his truck in the area."

"Yeah. Kind of like the mail carrier," I said.

"Exactly."

"I wonder why Daemon and Ruston didn't blow up the place while it was vacant?" she mused.

"Daemon said, Ruston wanted the house back. What better way to stop offers than to make mischief? No one who knew the history would bid on it. The only other offer was from a thin, older woman with a big nose," I mused, sipping wine.

"Ruston's mother!" I said. We gasped and looked at each other.

Rap. Rap. We jumped.

"Are you expecting someone?" Myra asked.

"No." I shook my head, went to the exit, and gazed out the peephole. "It's Don," I said, puzzled. After a long minute, I walked away. I was done. I never wanted to see or talk to Don Williams again.

"You won't let him in?" She asked, her eyebrows raised.

"Nope."

"Katelyn. I hear you in there. Please. Open the door," Don's voice came.

I ignored him and filled my glass, offering Myra a refill. We rolled our eyes and snickered.

"Katelyn. Please. I have a pizza. It is your favorite. Hawaiian."

I grinned at Myra, leaped up, flew to the entry, and threw it open. "Why didn't you say so?"

I snatched the box from his hands and shut the door in his face.

"Katelyn Baxter!" Myra admonished me.

"Oh, okay!" I opened the entry and stood aside, letting him pass. He sat next to Myra on the couch.

"Good to see you, Myra."

"You, as well, Sheriff," she said. "My brother is good, thank you."

I groaned, headed to the cupboard, and took out plates for pizza. Amid taking out dishes, there was another knock, then Eddy's voice, "Hey, Wifey? Are you there?"

I smirked and let Eddy in.

His dark hair tousled, deep brown eyes twinkling, he surveyed Myra and Don.

"Hey, Myra. Hey Sheriff."

"Eddy," Don said, coolly. The two men viewed each other. Myra smiled mischievously as she looked from me to Don, and then to Eddy.

"Want some pizza, Eddy?"

"That would be great, Kate. I'll help."

"Okay." Speechless, I retreated to the kitchen. Eddy followed, and in the back of my conscience, the words from “No Such Thing as a Broken Heart” by Old Dominion ran through my mind.

CHAPTER 26

It was a warm and breezy September day, and the anticipation of a long, glorious fall was in the air. It was dusk when Myra and I visited the site of the Hiptown house. I had driven to her home, and she drove to what remained. Together, we stood on the side of the vacant lot in companionable silence and surveyed the plot. A few trees had survived the explosion. Notably, the oak tree remained. It had stood strong through the lightning strike and the explosion. It had turned a deep crimson red, with leaves about to drop.

Both the house and garage were destroyed. The fire had traveled from the home to the garage, making the out building a loss. The planting area where Skye had been found was covered with fallen maple leaves.

"Myra, you're *sure* you want to build on the lot?" I had sold the land to Myra, vowing never to renovate a dwelling outside of Crocus Heights again. Best to know the neighborhood.

"Yes. It will be perfect!" she said, her eyes glowing with excitement. Construction would start the next day. The foundation was dug, ready for new basement concrete.

"Awaaaaaillll" A low yowl came, rose, and ended in a deafening note.

"What was that?" I gasped, scanning the area.

"Awaaaaaillll" the howl echoed and reverberated.

"It sounds like it's coming from over there." I inhaled, shuddered, and pointed to the back of the home site, closest to where the garage had been. Myra's face slumped, and her complexion paled in the dim light. She stood ramrod straight, still, listening.

"OMG!" I gasped. "Myra. That's the sound I heard when I was trapped in the basement. This place is still haunted!"

"Let's get out of here," she whispered.

"You got it!"

"Awaaaaaillllll! Awaaaaaaillll!"

THE END

KATELYN'S HOME IMPROVEMENT TIPS

For an easy homemade wood polish, mix 1 cup of water, 1 cup vinegar, 1 T olive oil in a spray bottle.

To make a heavy-duty wood cleaner, mix 3 T. olive oil with 1 T. vinegar. Wipe on, wipe off.

Use 1 cup of white vinegar in place of fabric softener to remove detergent build up and soften towels every few weeks.

Use 1/2 cup baking soda with regular laundry detergent to soften towels.

For pesky weeds, mix a gallon of vinegar, a cup of salt or borax, with 1 T. of dish soap. Spray and repeat.

Straight lemon juice (like ReaLemon) in a spray bottle also works on weeds.

To prevent critters from taking up residence in your home, block any openings, install chimney caps, vent covers, etc. Trim tree branches that allow creatures to travel to the roof and gain entry to your home.

To eliminate mice: set up traps, block openings, or try the traditional method of mouse removal—a cat.

Call in a professional to remove wild animals, like raccoons. Momma might be protecting her young.

Rugs and carpeting will cut down on everyday household noise. A fan or sound machine provides white noise and may help with unwanted sounds.

There are professional water removal companies that can help with a basement flood. Otherwise, there is the DIY method of muscle and rental machines.

The same holds true for refinishing floors. Rental sanding machines and muscle.

Home is nice. Make yours as nice as you can.

ACKNOWLEDGEMENTS

Thank you to Betty Borns for your faith, friendship, and laughter through the chapters of our lives.

Thank you to Judith Anne Horner and Joe Sebesta for beta reading DEADLY FLIP. Your insights made it a better novel.

Thank you to the Word Whippers Critique Group: William Anderson, Cathlene Buchholtz, Dale Butler, Barb Danson, and Mary Rodgers for their continuing support of this series.

Thank you to Julie Seedorf, and all my sisters and brothers at SINC, Twin Cities Chapter, and the Guppies group for their fellowship, advice, and support.

ABOUT THE AUTHOR

M. E. Bakos has published several short stories in national women's magazines. Her love of mysteries has led to writing cozies. Her first mystery short story, "Carpe Diem or Murder at the Carp Fest" appeared in the *Festival of Crime: a SINC Anthology*. Her second, "Perfect Storm . . . Perfect Murder" is published in *Dark Side of the Loon*, May, 2018, also a SINC Anthology.

She is an enthusiastic fan of home improvement shows and has done numerous home projects through the years. A fun fact: she interned with a Minneapolis non-profit housing agency, where she researched, wrote, and edited a monthly home improvement newsletter.

She is a member of Twin Cities Sisters in Crime, the SINC Guppies Group, and an alumna of the University of Minnesota.

She lives with her husband, Joe Sebesta, and their spoiled Morkie (Maltese/Yorkie), Chipper, in Minnesota.

Thank you for reading DEADLY FLIP, A Home Renovator Mystery.

If you liked the novel, please review on your favorite retail site. Your feedback is always welcome and greatly appreciated. Email: mebakos@yahoo.com or visit: https://mebakos.wixsite.com/author.

Books in this series:

FATAL FLIP, Book 1
DEADLY FLIP, Book 2
LETHAL FLIP, Book 3

www.ingramcontent.com/pod-product-compliance
Ingram Content Group UK Ltd.
Pitfield, Milton Keynes, MK11 3LW, UK
UKHW041637190726
13854UKWH00006B/2540

9 798985 077070